TAUL LAVNE

Oct. 14 — 1
15 — 2
16 — 3
17 — 4
18 — 5
19 — 6
20 — 7
21 — 8
22 — 9
23 — 10
24 — 11
25 — 12
26 — 13
27 — 14
28 — 15
29 — 16
30 — 17
31 — 18
Nov. 1 — 19
Nov. 2 — 20
Nov. 3 — 21
" 4 — 22

THE LONE RANGER
and
The Gold Robbery

No. 3

The Lone Ranger Stories

Written by

FRAN STRIKER

and based on the famous
Lone Ranger adventures
created by

GEO. W. TRENDLE

The Lone Ranger
and the Gold Robbery

Written by FRAN STRIKER

and based on the famous *Lone Ranger* adventures

created by GEO. W. TRENDLE

GROSSET & DUNLAP *Publishers*

NEW YORK

CONTENTS

THE LONE RANGER
and the Gold Robbery

CHAPTER I

"A Masked Man's Ride."

Fog swirled and eddied behind the backs of the two horsemen as they left a small promontory to descend into the vague shadows of the valley. Ahead, mist hung heavy in the twilight above an almost tropical mass of rank vegetation that grew in tangled madness from a black ooze of slimy muck.

Since daybreak, the pair had been in the saddle, pausing only long enough to water their horses, and soak their bandannas in water holes to wipe away the trail dust mixed with sweat. To reach their destination, the town of Black River, by the following morning, meant riding steadily and in as straight a line as possible. The weird stories of "The Devil's Bog" . . . strange tales of mystery that shrouded the swale of reeking undergrowth and treacherous quicksand, were not enough to deter the Lone Ranger and his

1

faithful Indian companion, Tonto, from their chosen route. To ride wide, and evade the region of the bog, meant many extra miles of travel. The Lone Ranger chose the direct way with characteristic disregard for obstacles, whether human or supernatural.

He couldn't, however, deny the eerie feeling of evil that gripped him as he neared the much-talked-of Devil's Bog. As he and Tonto came nearer, a horrible stench of rotting things filled the air. The water of the bog was stagnant, covered with a thick scum of sickly-looking green, broken only by the bubbles of marsh gas that rose from the muck of the bottom. The only sound, other than the rhythm of the hoofbeats, was the steady drone of buzzing flies and the twilight croaking of frogs. These sounds seemed to increase the air of desolation about the place . . . to make the silence even more gripping and mysterious.

Tonto glanced toward his left where the setting sun formed long ghostlike shadows of the dead trees which thrust their gaunt skeletons like grim, grey sentinels above the smaller, living growth. There was no breeze to stir the weeds and grasses. When they moved, it was because of the passage of small crawling things, moving through the swamp. The atmosphere was thick, sticky and humid.

Even the gallant Silver, the horse of the Lone Ranger, seemed to feel the oppressive atmosphere. His ears lay back against his head and he seemed apprehensive, ready at any moment to move with all the lightning speed of his great muscles, to dodge an unknown adversary.

"Everyone," explained the Lone Ranger to Tonto, "avoids the Devil's Bog."

The Indian turned attentively toward the masked speaker.

"There are a lot of strange stories told about this place. It seems that any number of men and horses have gone into it, never to come out again. Some of the stories are just campfire tales, but . . . ," he paused and his voice softened, "SOME of the stories are true."

Tonto nodded slowly. He knew how the vivid imagination of cowmen and sheepherders could enhance the smallest item of fact until it became a lurid tale of adventure to be repeated, and further expanded, at every campfire. But Tonto also knew that there was plenty of truth in the yarns of lost souls in the Devil's Bog. The Indians, long before the advent of the white men, had feared and avoided the place. Tonto's own people had their legends about the bog, just as did the white men.

"The explanation is simple," went on the masked man as he led his horse ever closer to the edge of still, viscous water. "It is quicksand."

That was the case. In almost the exact center of the bog there was an island of firm ground, surrounded by the quicksand. Among other amazing stories were several concerning treasure buried on the island. Of those who had tried to find the treasure, many were sucked down by the quicksand, and finally the last attempt had been made, and abandoned. Though no treasure had ever been found, or even sought for, for a number of years, the rumors of the treasure still persisted.

In many parts of the West, the Lone Ranger was a familiar figure, but he was heading for Black River for the first time. The mask that covered the entire upper half of his face, would have hampered most men in a hand-to-hand fight, or a running attack against the odds the Lone Ranger was so frequently called upon to meet. But the mask was a part of the tall, lean-hipped, broad-shouldered man. He wore it even when there was no likelihood of being seen. He sometimes wore it when he slept. His face, from the brim of the large white sombrero to just above the firm, well-shaped lips and determined chin, felt strange without the mask. There were times, in his past adventures, when the mask would have aroused unwelcome questions, and only at times like this did he remove it. Even then his own face was not shown; he carefully disguised himself with stains and dyes, all concocted by Tonto from roots, herbs and berries.

Silver, all his senses tuned to a high pitch, gave a soft, warning whinny. At first the Lone Ranger thought it was nothing but the dreariness of the place, but when the sound was twice repeated, he knew there was something ahead, something that was not in keeping with the solitude. Kneeing Silver slightly, the Lone Ranger drew closer to Tonto. He whispered a few words, and Tonto squinted into the haze ahead, shading his eyes from the red glow of the western sky. After a moment he shook his head slowly. "Silver wrong," he muttered, "nothing on trail ahead."

Tonto had traveled with the Lone Ranger ever since that day long past, when the white man was the sole survivor of an attack which wiped out an entire band of Texas Rangers. The Lone Ranger, a member of the band, was badly wounded. His injuries would probably have killed him if it hadn't been for Tonto. For it was Tonto, a wandering Indian, who found him and nursed the faint spark of life back to a glowing flame of vigorous health.

Then, so the killers would not know him as a survivor of the band of Texas Rangers, the white man masked his face. With Tonto at his side, he fought the marauders to avenge the death of his friends, and rid the state of Texas of a choking yoke of outlawry.

Time after time, he rode down on the killers. He

captured some of them himself, as they skirmished away from the main band. Others, he brought the lawmen to arrest. Each time, when his hard riding and thrilling courage brought others of the outlaw band to justice, he rode away without awaiting thanks, or reward. His identity was never learned. Finally, the last of those who had battled and killed the Lone Ranger's partners, was lodged in jail to await a trial, and ultimately to hang.

Then, his work in Texas finished, he found himself known only as the Lone Ranger and recognized as a power of strength in the name of justice . . . a grim nemesis to outlaws, however daring. The stories of his exploits spread throughout the West, and he became an almost legendary character with his mighty stallion, said to be the most powerful horse in seven states. Tonto was constantly at his side, and the buckskin clothes, the black hair drawn to a tight war-knot behind his head, and the red band that circled his head at the brow, were as familiar as the masked man and his horse, or as his ringing cry of "Hi-Yo Silver!"

Tonto had traveled many a trail with the masked rider, and his strength, added to a matchless skill with gun or rope, and the quick mind of the Lone Ranger, made them an incomparable pair. All the lore of past generations was stored in Tonto's mind. He possessed an animal-like sense in following a trail that was invisible to the white man's eyes. His knowledge of medicine, like that of his forefathers, was crude but effective. He knew all the moods of nature.

The Lone Ranger seemed spurred on his hunt for outlaws by a burning desire to see justice done. No one knew where he came from or where he went, and none knew what fuel fired his determination to aid the oppressed and discouraged, and seek punishment for the lawless.

This bond of friendship between the two was rare indeed. The Lone Ranger's great love for the West brought about his desire to see it conquered and settled, and made prosperous. It was for this, that he did all he could to help those who came into the West to live. Tonto too loved the West, and hoped the day would come when redman and white could lay aside their weapons and live together in peace. This mutual devotion to the country, an admiration for strength and courage, and the obvious fact that each was the complement of the other, welded the masked man and the Indian into a companionship that would survive as long as life itself.

It was indeed a rare event for either Silver or Tonto to be mistaken, but one of them was certainly wrong now. While Tonto, keen though his eyes might be, saw nothing ahead at which to be alarmed, Silver's every motion told of apprehension.

"We'll be past the bog in a few minutes," the Lone Ranger called to Tonto, "and then there's nothing but open plain between us and Black River."

"Get-um by Devil Bog before dark," replied the Indian. "That good."

The masked man too felt relieved when he was sure they would put the grim place behind them before total darkness shrouded the plain, but then he noticed that Silver, who had been given a slack rein all day, was shortening his stride.

"Come on, Silver!" he called. The horse, usually obedient to the masked man, and only to the masked man, now refused to accept the command. He slowed to a walk, and Tonto was forced to draw in his paint to keep abreast.

Something other than the nature of the place had impressed the big white horse. Despite the resonant commands of the Lone Ranger, the horse stubbornly slowed down, and finally stopped. His ears cocked forward, and he stood stiff-legged, every motion arrested, save the nervous rippling of the splendid muscles beneath their coat of gleaming white. And then the Lone Ranger heard the sound.

CHAPTER II

"A MANHUNT BEGINS."

At first, the Lone Ranger thought it was some animal who made the faint, plaintive sound, but when it was repeated, he recognized it as the cry of a man in the last stages of despair, calling for help. Tonto heard it too, and his keen senses correctly placed the direction of the sound. Then he saw the head of a man, almost invisible in the haze, just beyond the edge of the bog. With a cry, he pointed, but already the Lone Ranger was in motion, as his hand snatched the rope from the saddle's pommel and whirled it in a loop above his head. Silver lunged ahead, his great strides carrying toward the one who had been sucked to his armpits in the hungry quicksand.

At close quarters, the reek of the bog was almost unbearable. When it seemed that Silver and the masked man would themselves plunge into the treacherous slime, the left hand of the Lone Ranger yanked hard on the reins, and brought the mighty stallion to a rearing halt. While sharp forefeet pawed the air, as Silver whirled, the masked man's loop snaked out with unerring aim. There was a gentle, muffled slap as the rope struck the water and splashed the green scum.

"Get the rope beneath your arms!" shouted the Lone Ranger, as he drew in the slack.

The man in the bog reached one hand, dripping with black ooze, and pawed at the rope. Each motion made him sink inches lower.

Tonto had dismounted, and stood ready to plunge into the swamp himself, if need be, and let the Lone Ranger drag him out while he in turn gripped the feebly struggling man who seemed barely able to help himself.

Again Ben Jenkins reached and this time he managed to get the lariat beneath one arm.

"Get the other arm above the rope," snapped the resonant voice. To Tonto, the Lone Ranger ordered, "Wait, he'll make it!"

The ringing confidence of that clear, sharp voice seemed to instill new strength into the man who had been so close to a wretched death. He got his other arm above the rope.

It took careful handling of the powerful Silver to drag the old fellow from the swamp, without doing it so suddenly that aged limbs might be snapped, or a shoulder dislocated. A slow, steady pull, and Jenkins' body moved toward the bog's edge. Slime clung to his clothes and streaked his face and iron-gray hair.

As if sobbing in lament over the loss of a victim, the hungry bog gave out a sucking sound as Jenkins finally was hauled to safety.

The old man was a pitiful object when he sprawled on solid ground, gasping for breath, and trembling in the thought of the death that had come so close. Hard lines grooved his weather-beaten face, his mustache dripped the foul liquid of the swamp and his breath came in laboured gasps. His movements were slow and painful, and he made no effort to get up from the ground.

Tonto wet a cloth from his canteen of clear water and wiped the scum and muck from Jenkins' face with a touch that was as gentle as that of any woman. The Lone Ranger, meanwhile, removed the rope, and with deft fingers examined the man for possible injuries.

He asked no questions. Instead he said, "Lie back and take it easy. It'll take a little while to get your breath. Don't try to talk yet."

The man's eyes closed, and a sigh of relaxation broke through his cracked, bloodless lips. After several minutes, he again looked at the two who'd saved him. His breathing was laboured, and becoming more so. Something more than the terror of the swamp was wrong. Then the masked man found it. The hole in Jenkins' shirt was hidden by the heavy, clinging layer of muck. It became apparent only when the red trickled through. Tonto saw the bullet wound at the same time, and as if he read the Lone Ranger's thoughts, the Indian took a knife from his belt and handed it to the white man.

In a few deft slashes, he cut away the shirt, and saw that the wound was a bad one, dangerously close to the heart. How dangerous, the masked man couldn't tell at once.

"Th . . . they got me," faltered the old man. His eyes were only half open, and the words seemed to hurt, as he formed them.

"Who shot you?" inquired the masked man softly.

"G . . . gold . . ."

"A man named Gold?"

Jenkins shook his head with an effort. "Lots . . . lots of gold . . . in . . . in the express . . . orfice."

Each motion brought more blood welling from the ugly wound. Tonto tried to staunch the flow, but his glance told the Lone Ranger that it was only a question of time, and that time but minutes, when the bullet would do what the quicksand had not done.

The Lone Ranger bent closer, his mouth close to the old man's ear. "Tell me," he urged, "who you are, and who shot you?"

Ben Jenkins gave his name, but disregarded the second question.

"J . . . Jenkins," he said. "I . . . I'm the one . . . the one that was tuh make the plans . . ." He paused for a full moment, struggling for the strength to carry on, "The plans for shippin' g . . . gold East . . ."

The Lone Ranger knew about that gold. His journey to Black River had been undertaken because of certain rumors concerning it.

"Let me save your breath," he told Ben Jenkins. "I'll tell you what I know, and you nod your head if I am right."

A feeble nod from Jenkins.

"At the express office in the town of Black River, there is over one hundred thousand dollars worth of bullion. That gold is to be sent to a broker in the East. A lot of outlaws in this part of the country would like to get their hands on it, so the shipping plans were to be kept secret!"

The old man nodded again. So far the Lone Ranger was right. He continued quickly, "You were to make all the arrangements, and only those who actually handled the gold were to know about those plans . . ."

Jenkins' breath came in gasps. He was slipping rapidly, and at any moment, it might be too late to gain information from him. The Lone Ranger spoke more rapidly, racing his words against the march of

Death itself. It was almost dark, too dark to see the varying expressions that swept across Ben Jenkins' face; expressions of pain, interspersed with eagerness to make his story known to this strong man who seemed to be a friend.

"We heard about the shipment, and thought there might be plans to steal it. That's why we were heading for Black River." Despite the speed of the masked man's words, he made himself clear to Jenkins. He felt, rather than saw, the nods of understanding. "To make the danger greater, the gold has to be started from Black River tomorrow, when the entire county celebrates Frontier Day. Hundreds of strangers will be in town, and any of those strangers might be the outlaws who plan to steal the gold!"

From that point on, the Lone Ranger had to guess, and he fervently hoped that Jenkins might live long enough to verify his guesses that were based on deduction: "Those who wanted the gold, knew you made the plans. They captured you, tortured you, and made you tell what the plans were."

For the first time, Jenkins shook his head in negation. I ... I ... didn't mean ... tuh tell 'em ..." he corrected.

"BUT YOU DID?"

"I ... I'm afeared ... when ... when I was only half conscious . . . they got it outen me." He spoke barely above a whisper. "I ... I sort of ... got half conscious, th ... then I seen ...," he paused again, then continued with greater difficulty, "I ... I seen that they was laughin', gloatin'. Then ... then they throwed me ... in the swamp ... an' rode off. One ... one of 'em turned back, an' throwed ... throwed a shot at me!" A fit of coughing seized him, his lean form shaking in a spasm. Tonto held the canteen to the old man's lips, but a sudden jerk knocked the water aside.

The Lone Ranger placed a firm arm under Jenkins' narrow shoulders and raised him to a sitting posture. Then a last cough brought red flecks from Ben's mouth, and the man went limp.

Silence, with only the creatures of the bog to break it, then slowly, gently, the masked man lowered the now still form to the ground. He felt for the pulse, and found it gone.

Tonto pointed slowly toward the faint glow on the distant horizon. The Lone Ranger nodded, "Gone West," he breathed.

He rose to his full height, and faced the direction Tonto pointed, while the Indian stood, slightly behind him, facing in the same direction.

From where he stood Tonto couldn't see his tall friend's face, but he noticed that while one hand removed the white Stetson, the other hand slipped off the mask. The Indian knew that now, as he stood there, his face unmasked and undisguised, and yet unseen, the Lone Ranger's eyes were closed, his head bowed, and his lips moving in a silent prayer. The Lone Ranger's tribute to a brave soul of the West, gone to the reward it so richly merited.

When the Lone Ranger turned to face his Indian friend, the mask was once more in place. His mouth was set in a grim line, and the steely-gray eyes were piercing, even in the gloom, as they showed from behind the slits. "Murdered," he breathed. "Murdered by men who know this swamp and are not afraid to come here. Murdered by men who will murder again, to get that gold."

The very softness of his voice, showed the strength of his determination, and Tonto knew, there on the plain between the dead form of Ben Jenkins, and the Devil's Bog, that neither he nor the Lone Ranger would rest until this murder had been avenged, its perpetrators punished, and one hundred thousand dollars worth of gold on its safe way to the East.

Tonto moved toward Scout, his paint horse. From the saddle he drew a short-handled spade. After the burial, the Lone Ranger would begin another man-hunt.

CHAPTER III

"The Lone Ranger Plans."

With the Devil's Bog and its eerie atmosphere behind them, the Lone Ranger and Tonto permitted their horses to lope in an easy, ground-covering gait across the moonlit plain as they continued on their way to Black River. Old Ben Jenkins had been given the crude but sincere ritual of a prairie burial, and his still form rested, wrapped in one of the masked man's blankets, several miles back. At first the Lone Ranger had intended to erect a small cross to mark the grave, but second thought changed his plans.

Certain outlaws, he knew, were planning to rob that fortune in gold that waited in Black River for shipment to the East. Those outlaws, if they returned to the bog and found the grave, would surmise that someone had taken Ben from the quicksand, and they might reason that he'd lived long enough to name his killers. "We'll return later," the Lone Ranger had said to Tonto, "and set a cross in place. Later, after we've finished our work here."

17

Tonto hadn't replied. The words of the Lone Ranger were the last spoken by either of the two for the better part of an hour. Phrases, gasped with Ben's last breath, kept running through the masked man's mind. He tried to piece them together, and grasp what the dying man was trying so hard to tell. He'd caught a name, Jack Bannerman. He gathered that Bannerman was the one in charge of shipping the gold, and felt, from what old Jenkins tried to say, that Bannerman could be trusted. Something had been said about the express office, and something more about the plans.

It was Tonto who broke the long silence. "What do-um in town?" the Indian inquired.

The same question must have been running through the masked man's mind. "I don't know," he answered frankly. "I don't know just how we can approach the situation in town." He paused for several minutes. "There are two men, I'm sure can be trusted. One is Jack Bannerman, the other one the Sheriff."

Tonto looked somewhat dubious at this statement. In his travels he'd seen many a lawman, working in close alliance with outlaws.

"The trouble is," continued the Lone Ranger, "I know what either one of them will say, if I approach them, masked as I am. They'll be on the lookout for anyone who looks the least suspicious. They'd think you and I were the ones who planned to steal the gold."

Tonto nodded agreement.

"Furthermore," continued the Lone Ranger, as if expressing his thought aloud as he made his plans, "If we tell anyone that Ben Jenkins is dead, it's quite possible that we'll be charged with his murder! Lawmen in this part of the country insist on hanging someone for every murder, and the sooner they hang someone, the sooner the murder is written off the books as solved."

"The plans, I think, are in the express office. Ben tried to tell me something about them, but I couldn't hear much of what he said. If we go to Bannerman, tell him Jenkins is dead, and tell him that Jenkins revealed the plans to outlaws, and ask him to CHANGE those plans, he'll feel that we want them changed, simply to make it easier to steal the gold. And yet, Tonto, those plans MUST BE CHANGED!" The last of the Lone Ranger's speech was made with emphasis.

In fact, his statement was so emphatic that Tonto looked at him sharply, knowing that a plan had already been formed in the Lone Ranger's mind. A plan, perhaps quite vague at present, but one which would undoubtedly involve a certain amount of danger.

The two continued toward the west, and Tonto noticed that their shadows made by the rising moon, were considerably shorter than they'd been a while ago. The moon was rising, and by its progress the Indian marked the time of night.

Quite suddenly, the Lone Ranger smacked one fist into the other palm. "It WILL work!" he announced. "Tonto, the first thing to do, is to prevent the theft of that gold, and the second, to find the killers of that old man. If the plans for shipping the gold are STOLEN, Bannerman will be sure to change them."

"That right," agreed the Indian.

"So," finished the Lone Ranger, "we will steal them!"

The simplicity of the scheme appealed to Tonto. It was, in fact, so simple that it could hardly fail to succeed. The written plans for shipment stolen, new plans would at once be made, and the gold shipped by a different route than that originally outlined. Thus the information gleaned by the torture of Ben Jenkins would be worthless to the outlaws. Moreover, if the Lone Ranger knew the ORIGINAL route, he might follow the stage and see what happened to it. If men tried to rob it, he would know those men as the murderers he wanted.

The Lone Ranger glanced toward the moon. "To make our plan succeed," he told the Indian, "we must reach Black River before daybreak and get those plans."

"Not far now," the Indian replied. "Make-um good time on trail."

It was true. Since leaving the Devil's Bog, the going had been easy, and the powerful horses were able to make far better time than either the Lone Ranger or Tonto had estimated when they started their long journey. The air was cool and crisp, and the horses seemed to gain fresh vigour as they progressed. "Instead of camping," said the Lone Ranger, "we'll push on for town. The sooner we get there, the better."

Tonto agreed, and heeled his horse hard. The paint lunged ahead. "Come on Silver!" cried the masked rider. He touched the big white stallion with an unspurred boot. Eager to race through that cool air, Silver surged ahead, passing the horse of the Indian. White mane and tail, lifted by the breeze, flew parallel to the ground. The brim of the masked man's hat flattened back against the high crown. His shirt filled and billowed on his back, as he leaned forward in the saddle.

As he pushed on toward Black River and the express office, where he hoped to find Ben Jenkins' carefully made plans, the Lone Ranger couldn't know that at that very moment, evil minds were plotting further deviltry.

CHAPTER IV

"Fate Intervenes."

When the annual Frontier Day celebration was held, the women and children of Black River stayed indoors. Men who couldn't handle their fists and guns, also found it wiser to remain indoors or stay away from the cafes and music halls. It was an occasion when the Sheriff simply crossed his fingers, swore in a dozen additional deputies, and told his men to try and prevent murder, but not to interfere in private fights.

From a sixty-mile radius, ranchers and cowboys came to Black River for the three-day celebration. They looked forward to a mighty whirlwind of revelry, contests, drinking and fun of the roughshod western sort. At the end of that time, they would return to their home ranches, exhausted, broke and happy. Though the holidays didn't officially open until the next afternoon, the early arrivals made the eve of the big affair a festive occasion. No one bothered to go to bed that first night.

The one main street, a narrow dirt road, was filled with men in all stages of intoxication, and more men jammed the stores and shops. Until daybreak, the barber shop would be well filled with men who were getting "scraped artistic" and their hair "cut an' curried proper."

The several restaurants which had been hastily opened in empty shacks for the occasion, did a land-office business by serving a rare delicacy known as "Cove Oysters." These oysters, a product of Maryland, came packed in sealed cans, and though an inferior product, they were greatly relished by the waddies. Probably because they appealed to the imagination more than to the palate.

Barbered and well-fed, it was the custom of the visitors to head for the nearest saloon, there to begin the serious business of the evening. In the largest of the saloons, however, there were three men who had time for neither the restaurants and their oysters, nor the barbers and the luxury of a professional shave. They were townsmen who seemed to have grim business at hand. Business that had no part in Frontier Day celebrating.

Their drinks stood untouched on the table. They kept their voices low, and not even the occasional blast of a six-gun, fired by some over-enthusiastic celebrant in the street outside, disturbed their conference.

In the center of the table, a cracked dish held a small heap of cigarette butts. All three of the men smoked incessantly, and none showed the slightest interest in the activity around them.

"I wonder," grumbled one of the trio, "if the old man gave us the true facts?"

The second man ground his cigarette against the rim of the well-filled dish. "Maybe we should have kept him alive until we made sure of what he told us," he said. "It would have been just like him to give us a bum steer."

The tallest of the sullen-looking trio hadn't spoken. He listened to his friends with a trace of amusement on his long, lean-joweled face.

"I don't think Jenkins could have thought up lies to tell us in the condition he was in," the first speaker murmured. "What do you think?" He addressed the tall man.

"When you two get through decidin' things, I'll tell you just WHAT we're goin' to do!"

The shifty-eyed pair looked with interest at the man between them.

"In the first place, it's best that Jenkins is dead. As long as he was alive, he could have squealed on us. Dead men don't talk."

"That's right," agreed one.

"In the second place, it doesn't matter whether he

told us the truth about those plans. I've changed my mind about takin' the gold, while it's bein' shipped."

"After all the trouble we went to to make Ben talk?"

"Yep, after all that trouble. We know where the gold is right now, and we might as well get it tonight, as to wait till tomorrow or next day."

"But," countered the man with the black hair, "we'd be takin' an awful risk, to try and get it from the safe in the express office!"

"No more risk, than to take the plans from that safe. It won't be hard to get away with the gold, not with the plan I have in mind."

"What's your plan?"

"A second man has to die!" He smirked slightly at the amazement on the others' faces. "But don't get excited until I tell you who that man is. Let's get going. We might just as well start now." He rose and heeled his chair away from the table. He tossed off the glass of fiery liquor in a single swallow, muttered "Here's luck!" and led the way outside.

Though the saloon was jammed with men, no one paid the slightest attention to the trio as the killers moved through the heavy fog of tobacco smoke and left the room.

Fate is a strange mistress, and on this night She was in one of her most conspiring moods. It must have been Fate who brought the Lone Ranger, a man who stood for honesty and fair dealing in the strictest sense of the word, into Black River that night with intentions of robbing certain papers from a desk in the express office. It must also have been Fate who put uncertainty into the killers' minds, and made them change their plans so that they went out to take the gold that night, instead of the following day.

But whether it was fate, coincidence, or just bad fortune, the Lone Ranger, in heading for the express office, was heading toward the greatest peril he had ever faced.

Arriving in town, the masked man and his Indian friend gave the lighted buildings and the crowded road wide berth. Though everyone was occupied with his own affairs, there were sure to be some who would notice, and wonder about, the man who wore a mask. Silently as shadows, the two moved behind the row of buildings. Raucous laughter, crude jokes, and maudlin songs reached their ears and drowned the faint sound of the horses' hoofs on the soft turf.

The moon had long since set; dawn was scarcely an hour away. Though both men had been in the saddle over twenty hours, save for the grim interlude at Devil's Bog, they showed no sign of fatigue. Their eagerness to complete their self-assigned task sustained them, and would sustain them for another day if need be.

The Lone Ranger could think of no reason why his plan to burglarize the express office should fail. He reasoned that Jack Bannerman would discover the robbery when he reported at his desk at nine that morning. By that time, the mask would be removed, and a disguise applied in its place, so the Lone Ranger could mingle with the crowds, and watch developments.

"The office," he whispered to Tonto, "is the last of this row of buildings."

Tonto saw the plain, one-story building with the stable in the rear. It stood at the end of the road, at right angles to the buildings on each side of the street. The wide veranda, one step off the ground, was covered by a roof, an extension of the roof of the building itself, to shelter those who might await the arrival of the stage coach. Four pillars, each one about a foot in thickness, supported that roof. It was a small but solidly constructed building, made to withstand the heavy windstorms of the section.

Dimly, beyond the edge of the big porch, the Lone Ranger and Tonto could see the door of the express office. They dismounted at one end of the porch. "Everyone keeps close to the cafes, Tonto," whispered the masked man, "I don't think we'll even be noticed."

"Take plenty care," cautioned Tonto, in spite of the masked man's words.

The Lone Ranger nodded, even though Tonto could hardly see his nod. Moving with the stealth of a panther, he stepped to the porch, and in a moment was close to the door, examining the padlock.

It was a heavy lock that went through an even heavier loop of iron on the door that coincided with another loop on the jam. The masked man removed his gloves, and examined the lock by touch, more than by sight. "Knife," he murmured.

Tonto placed a knife in the masked man's hand for a second time that night, and a gentle scraping told of the efforts to pick the lock. Justified though he was in what he did, the Lone Ranger felt a sense of guilt in forcing an entry into that office.

Tonto watched intently with his back to the Lone Ranger. The distant light from the saloons and torches in the street, reflected softly from his bronzed face. His ears were strained to catch the click that would inform him that the lock was sprung, and that his tall white friend was ready to enter the stout building. The sound that DID come, was not a click. It was a crash like that of thunder, but even sharper. Tonto knew that sound. It was the blast of a heavy gun in close quarters, and it was followed by the scream of a human, in the throes of death. Both shot and scream, came from just beyond that door where the Lone Ranger stood!

CHAPTER V

"Stolen Gold."

The scream that froze both the Lone Ranger and Tonto to stark rigidity on the broad veranda of the express office, was without sex. It came from beyond the door where he'd been working at the lock but whether the voice was that of man or woman, he couldn't tell.

Close behind the scream, a heavy gun roared in the confines of the office, then the sound of breaking glass.

It seemed for a moment that time stood still. Countless thoughts and impressions flashed through the mind of the Lone Ranger in the seconds he stood there, tense, listening. That shot and the scream were louder than any noise he'd make by splintering the door in a more drastic entrance than he'd intended. If anything would arouse the men in the street, near the torchlights, they had already been aroused. The need now was speed, not secrecy. Perhaps there'd be a fight when he gained the inside of the office. If so, he must conquer and find the plans he sought in time to make his escape.

He tossed the knife to Tonto, shouting "Take it." Then snatching one of his heavy guns, he stepped back a pace and lunged hard at the heavy door. It shook, but held firm.

The Lone Ranger didn't waste time or bullets trying to smash that heavy lock. He felt it would be useless. He drew back a second time, then threw himself with all his weight and power. The impact hurt his shoulder, and sent jarring pain shooting through his entire side, but the screws of the hinges ripped from the wood. Released on the side opposite the lock, the door swung in with the masked man, who was carried on into the office by the force of his drive, struggling to keep his feet. He recovered quickly, and cast a hurried look around him.

The room was dark, the only light, a faint glow of the flares near the cafes, came through the now-opened door. The acrid odor told the masked man that the shot had been fired in this room, but whoever fired it, must have fled by the rear door which was slightly ajar. The room was empty.

Quick strides took the Lone Ranger to the half-opened door, but he couldn't see through the darkness. He felt Tonto touch his arm and heard the Indian say, "You hurry!"

"What's the matter? Was the shot heard down at the saloon?"

"That right."

The Indian pointed toward the men a quarter of a mile away. Instead of the boisterous fun, and gay shouts, that had characterized them a moment ago, the group advancing toward the express office showed grim purpose in their movements.

"Come here, see what shot mean."

"Tonto, you'll have to stand them off long enough to give me a chance to find the plans."

"Tonto do."

"Get your rifle from Scout, and stand in the shelter of one of the pillars."

Tonto was gone, racing across the porch to the far end where the horses stood. The Lone Ranger swung back inside. He heard the men's loud shouts.

"They're after the express office," one fellow yelled.

Another voice cried, "Head 'em off." The rest was lost in the hubbub that came closer every second.

There was so much to be learned, and scant seconds in which to learn it. But first of all, he knew, the Lone Ranger must find those plans. Then, if possible, the source of that terror-stricken scream.

More accustomed to the darkness now, the Lone Ranger's eyes found the big iron safe. Two steps took him to it, and a glance showed it open and empty. The gold was gone and boxes and papers were scattered about the floor.

Oblivious to the men outside, and only vaguely aware of the ring of Tonto's rifle, and the distant response of six-guns, the Lone Ranger concentrated every faculty on the task at hand. Beads of perspiration stood on his face while his hands felt the inside of the safe to verify the absence of the gold.

He had to have a light, regardless of the risk. Raking a match on his boot-heel, he held the flame close to the floor, and scanned the papers quickly. Old receipts, account forms, waybills and other equipment and records of transactions; all of which were meaningless. Then, he spied a brown envelope with a wax seal over the flap. Of all things on the floor, this was the only one that held any likelihood of being the plans he wanted. He stuffed it in his pocket and stood erect.

By the last of the burning match, he made a quick survey of the room. There was no sign of anyone, wounded or dead. Aside from a lamp, broken on the floor beside the table, everything seemed in order save for the looted safe. He dropped the match and stepped on it, then made for the door, and Tonto.

The Indian was firing as fast as he could load and pull the trigger. The leader of the approaching men shouted to spread out and attack the express office from all sides. As he gave the order he emptied his gun toward the pillar that protected the Indian.

Lead slugs chugged into the post and front wall of the building. Other guns spouted orange flame. It would be impossible to withstand that fire for long, especially with the townsmen spreading out, to close in from the sides as well as the front.

As the Lone Ranger came through the door, he emptied both guns over the townsmen's heads. The men fell back momentarily at the sudden fusillade from a new source. "Now's our chance!" yelled the masked man. "To the horses, Tonto!"

The Indian obeyed, his moccasined feet making hardly a sound as he led the way to the porch's end, closely followed by the Lone Ranger, who reloaded his guns as he ran.

The men, seeing that only two made up the party of what they thought were outlaws, recovered their formation, and with more gunfire and shouting, again moved toward the fugitives.

Dan Potter himself, the Sheriff of the county, led the attack. When he saw the horses for the first time, he let out a howl of "Get 'em, don't let 'em git away. They robbed the express office." He fired blindly, hoping to hit either of the men, or one of the horses, as he heard the ringing shout of the masked man, "Hi-Yo Silver."

The white horse leaped away, as if sprung from a

catapult. The paint horse was close behind it. Dan Potter's hammer fell on empty cartridges, and with fervent curses, he jammed fresh shells into his weapon's magazine. "The rest of yuh fire on him," he screamed to his companions, but they too had to reload. When Dan Potter was ready to fire again, both men and horses were gone. He saw nothing, though he still heard the receding beat of hoofs, and once again he heard the ringing cry, "Hi-Yo Silver, Away," with the last syllable drawn out, floating back to him, on the crisp night air.

Barking orders to certain of the men to get their horses and start on the trail of the two who'd left in such a hurry, Dan Potter himself, went inside the looted office, taking a couple of men with him.

He struck a match, and reached for the lamp in its familiar place on a desk. "Darn," he barked, when he saw the remains of the shattered lamp on the floor. There was another lamp on a table though, so he lighted this and then stood there, surveying the scene.

Though Sheriff Potter was a high-strung, quick-tempered old fire-eater, and though his grey mustache would bristle at the slightest inconvenience, he became calm, and entirely self-possessed when he faced a genuine catastrophe, or real danger.

The sight of the empty safe, the scattered papers, and the broken door, told their own story. "Boys," began the lawman in a soft, steady voice, "they've got the gold."

Murmurs of astonishment swept over the dozen men. All had known of the gold, but none knew where it was being held. None, except Sheriff Potter, and those who had to be taken into the secret.

"But they ain't got away with it yet," continued Potter. "Not by a darn sight. I got a pretty fair look at them two as they headed fer their hosses, an' they ain't no one from around here. One of 'em wore a mask, an' his sombrero was white. The other one was an Indian an' both were over six feet tall. We're goin' tuh start the biggest manhunt this county's ever seen, an' they ain't none of you deputies goin' tuh rest until that gold's brought back."

Mutters of agreement accepted the Sheriff's decision.

"Now all of yuh git yer hosses, arm yerselves tuh the teeth, an' be ready tuh start out at daybreak. That gives you half an hour to git ready!"

The crowded room emptied itself, as the men left in two's and three's, eager and anxious to be on the trail of the pair they had every reason to believe had robbed the office. There were queries as to the shot they heard, and the scream that brought them on the run, but Sheriff Potter, they knew, would follow up these angles. With satisfaction several of the regular deputies noted the soft, muddy condition of the ground. It wouldn't be a hard task to run down the Lone Ranger and Tonto.

Moreover, though none of the posse knew it, the Lone Ranger and Tonto, and their horses, were in no condition for a long, hard trip.

CHAPTER VI

"INTO THE DEVIL'S BOG."

There was a limit to the strength of even the mighty white stallion, Silver. The Lone Ranger had pushed hard, after leaving the town of Black River and the express office. Tonto's smaller horse, he knew, couldn't maintain the pace much longer.

They were riding directly into the rising sun, just as they'd ridden into the red glow of the sun the night before when they headed in the opposite direction.

There wasn't the slightest doubt in the mind of either of the fugitives regarding their position. They had been seen by Sheriff Dan Potter and a score of other men when they fled from the express office shortly after a shot and a scream brought the townsmen on the run. No amount of argument could convince the lawmen that they were not the ones who had looted the safe. They had gone there to steal. The Lone Ranger had been willing to be charged with the theft of the plans for the shipment of gold, in view of the story he could tell, and back with proof, in the form of Ben Jenkins' grave, and the outlaws he hoped to capture. Now all this was changed. He himself was the one to be charged with the theft of the gold and when the murder of Jenkins was learned, he would unquestionably be accused of that as well. The real killers would see to that. The Fate that had sent the Lone Ranger to the scene of the robbery had put him into their hands as a pawn. There was no way to prove his innocence. Once captured, he would hang, and Tonto with him.

These thoughts brought lines of worry into the strong face of the masked man. No words were exchanged between him and the faithful Indian who rode beside him. Each man was busy with his thoughts, and those thoughts were almost identical. It wasn't fear of death, or worry for himself that bothered the Lone Ranger. It was the worry that the real outlaws would escape unpunished if the crime were to be marked "closed" with a double hanging! The Lone Ranger and Tonto were the only two men alive, who knew that SOMEONE other than themselves had killed Ben Jenkins, stolen the gold, and fired a shot that must certainly have struck someone in the express office, despite the fact that there had been no dead form there.

"Tonto," he said finally. The Indian looked toward him, his face showing fatigue, and his eyes bloodshot with the glare of the morning sun. "We must find a place to rest our horses."

"There is a posse after us. They'll have no trouble in following our trail."

"That right."

Tonto looked behind him. The trail was clearly marked, and even more damning than he'd thought. There was a double set of tracks. The tracks made when he and the Lone Ranger had ridden toward Black River during the night, and the tracks showing their return. The lawmen could reach no other conclusion, than that they'd gone to town for no other purpose than to commit robbery.

"Where hide-um?" asked the Indian.

"There is just one place near enough to reach, and we may die getting into that place."

Tonto looked somewhat curious at the Lone Ranger's statement.

"The Devil's Bog!"

Tonto slowly shook his head from left to right. "No man reach-um there alive." He paused a moment, and then told what the Lone Ranger already knew. "Quicksand there. That plenty bad."

"But there's a small island of firm land in the center of the bog, Tonto. There is SOME way to reach that island. We're going to do our level best to find it. The posse won't have any trouble following us. We're leaving plain enough tracks. There isn't any hard rock near here, and there are no streams of water. There's no way to hide our tracks. If we go to the bog, the lawmen may think we've perished in the quicksand."

"Mebbe that what happen," interrupted Tonto.

"But there's a chance that we'll come out of the bog alive, Tonto. We've no choice. We must take that chance. If we don't live, or if we're captured, there will be no hope of having Justice served."

"Mebbe fight-um lawmen."

"We can't do that Tonto. We'd have to shoot some of those men. We would be captured in the end, anyway. Then no one would believe our story. No, Tonto, our only hope is to stay out of the hands of the law until we find the real crooks and get proof of their guilt."

As they rode, both men cast frequent glances behind them, not knowing how soon the Sheriff and his men might break into view, thundering toward them with guns blazing.

The plans for the shipment of the gold were in the Lone Ranger's pocket, the right breast-pocket of his shirt. He could feel the crinkle of the paper with each motion of his horse. He hadn't even bothered to look at the plans. They were meaningless, now that the gold had been taken.

The memory of the gunshot and the frantic scream in the office of the express company, bothered him. He was sure a bullet had found its mark. Yet, in the momentary flash of light, when he struck the match, he had seen no sign of the bullet's victim. He couldn't understand it. He felt some vague uncertainty; something that wasn't right about the scene there in the office. He tried to recall small details of the place. No chance for anyone on the floor to have been concealed by the table. The desk was hard against the wall. No room behind it. A couple of chairs and filing cabinets just about completed his mental inventory of the fixtures in the place. "He might have," he murmured, "been dragged through the back door." For a time he considered this possibility. It WAS a possibility, but hardly a probability. A man, when shot, falls down. Even though the wound isn't a fatal one, the impact of a .44 would spin a man, then drop him. Judging by the volume of the report he heard, the gun was no smaller than a .44. Had the man been shot, fallen, and been dragged from the place, a trail of red stain, would have been almost inevitable. "There is," he finished musingly, "something mighty curious about that shout, and the scream, something that should be investigated."

The sun was high and scorching hot. Though every moment counted in the ride for the Devil's Bog, Tonto and the Lone Ranger had to pause at increasingly frequent intervals to rest their almost staggering horses.

At about noon, during a pause beside a small spring, the Lone Ranger expressed some surprise that the lawmen hadn't already come into view.

"Mebbe keep-um on past bog," suggested Tonto. "Maybe lawmen not find-um trail."

"And keep on going?"

"That right."

"We can't Tonto. If we continue toward the East, we'll be too far from Black River. Remember, as soon as this chase is over, and we've given the horses a rest, we've got to go back to town. We left a lot of things unfinished there."

Tonto, instead of replying, slapped the spotted neck of his paint. The horse lifted its dripping muzzle from the spring, and seemed ready to go on. Tonto wouldn't admit it, not even to the Lone Ranger, but fear of the Devil's Bog was a heritage, handed down from many generations of his people.

Tonto would evade the bog, if possible. If not, he'd conquer his fear, and keep it suppressed. The Indian had true courage. It isn't courage, to know no fear. Courage, is the ability to go on, in spite of fear.

Silver finished a long, cooling drink, and then the dust-covered, travel-worn men and horses started once again toward the Devil's Bog, a place of horrible death, or refuge, and they didn't know which it might be.

Sheriff Potter's eagerness proved his undoing at the start of the pursuit. Despite the suggestion of a couple of his men, he was determined to start after the masked man and the Indian, as soon as possible, instead of waiting for better light. As a result, he made a false start. The twilight of dawn was deceiving, and the tracks he followed were the wrong ones.

By the time the posse corrected the mistake, and finally found the right trail, an hour's time had been lost. As it was, Sheriff Potter came into sight of the fugitives and the Devil's Bog, at about the same time. He let out a shout to his men, "There they are boys, we got 'em now!"

Half a dozen shouts clipped the air. Instinctively the members of the posse spurred their horses, anxious to end the chase, and bending low in the saddle, each man snatched his six-gun or carbine from its scabbard, ready to drill the pair ahead, at the first sign of resistance.

"Hold yer fire," commanded Sheriff Potter. "I want 'em alive, if possible."

Like bloodhounds, who bark when the quarry is in sight, or hunting dogs when they finally tree the fox, the men's voices whooped almost continuously as they thundered closer to the Lone Ranger and Tonto.

Then a new tone changed their voices. All the men saw the Lone Ranger's purpose at the same time. It was the Sheriff who shouted; "He's headin' fer the bog. Don't let him git in there. We can't chase him there. Start shootin'!"

To emphasize his words, Potter blazed with his gun. At the range, he had no hope of hitting the mark. He didn't even aim. But the action brought a volley of rifle fire from the men behind him. As fast as they could load and trigger their guns, the lawmen blazed toward the distant pair.

They let their horses have their heads, using both hands to handle their weapons. It was long-range shooting, and aiming was impossible from the rising and falling saddles, but despite these things, the lead slugs spurted dust from the ground, uncomfortably close to the Lone Ranger and his Indian friend.

"If this bog were another half mile, we'd never have made it." The Lone Ranger pulled hard, to swing the big white stallion directly toward the bog. There wasn't time to investigate the edge of the sluggish water. No time to hunt firm footing. He and Tonto must get into that swale without delay.

"Dismount," he barked, as he swung to the ground. Tonto did so. "One chance in a hundred that we'll come through this alive, Tonto. There's no use taking the lives of our horses with our own."

"That right."

Leaving their horses for the Sheriff to pick up, and

hoping those great beasts would be given the kind of treatment good horseflesh deserves, the two pushed tall reeds aside, and plunged into the thick, green-coated water of the Devil's Bog.

CHAPTER VII

"A State of Siege."

The Lone Ranger and Tonto sank to their knees
at their first steps into the bog. The muddy bottom
gripped their ankles and both expected momentarily
to feel themselves sucked down by the quicksand.

"If," the masked man said, "we can reach that small
island, there is just one slim chance that we'll come
through this alive."

"That right."

"But we've got to get far enough into this swamp,
to be concealed by the grass behind us. Otherwise,
the Sheriff's men will see us."

They waded in water halfway between their knees
and hips. Though they could feel their feet sink several inches with every step, they hadn't yet struck
quicksand.

"If you feel quicksand, Tonto," instructed the
masked man, "throw yourself flat. You don't sink as
fast that way, and you might be able to squirm out."

"Tonto know-um."

46

The swamp was a nightmare of mud and water that reeked of the decayed, almost tropical vegetation. What beauty there was, was horrible. Brightly colored dragon flies buzzed and droned on every side, and other varicolored insects glistened as the sun reflected from their tiny bodies with a myriad of gleaming colors.

The two men heard the Sheriff's posse clatter to a halt when they were halfway to the island. They were concealed from view, but the moving reeds and grasses might betray them. The angry curses of the men on shore filled the air, and from some of the things that were said, the Lone Ranger knew that Silver and Scout had been found and captured. He could hear the Sheriff's admiring comments on the horses, and once more hoped that if this marked the end of the trail for him and Tonto, the horses that had been such gallant friends, would be given the treatment such horseflesh deserved.

Then gunfire started. Bullets clipped and zoomed through the bog. Tonto glanced back.

He couldn't see the shore. It was unlikely then, that the lawmen had seen him. As if reading the Indian's thought, the Lone Ranger spoke, "They can't spot us. They're just firing at random, hoping a bullet may catch us."

Tonto nodded.

The two pressed on, during another volley of gun-fire, and then silence.

"Wait a minute," whispered the Lone Ranger, "I want to hear what the Sheriff is going to do."

He stood still, trying hard to ignore the stinging flies.

"There ain't a man in a million can go in there an' not die." It was Sheriff Potter speaking, "But I don't aim to take no chances."

The Lone Ranger wondered if the grim manhunter would follow into the swamp. If he did . . . then there could be only one thing to follow. A fight, a hand-to-hand struggle in which one or more must die. His lips compressed into a bloodless line as he stood tense, listening.

"One man in a million," he repeated, "An' mebbe the masked man's the one! I don't aim to leave here without him!"

A large gnat settled on the cheek of Tonto. The Lone Ranger saw the insect and knew the motionless Indian felt the pain of the sting, but endured it in stoic silence, rather than rustle the grass by moving, and thus betray their presence.

"It'd be foolhardy," went on the Sheriff, "fer us tuh try an' follow them two intuh the swamp. Instead of that, we'll surround the place, an' starve 'em out, if they're still alive."

"Ain't much chance o' them bein' alive in THERE," said someone.

"Just the same, we ain't takin' the chance of the gold thieves gettin' away. I seen 'em hit fer the swamp, an' they went empty-handed. They didn't take no vittles with 'em, an' they ain't nothin' they can eat inside there. Not even a berry. We'll camp right here an' a couple of the boys'll ride fer grub."

"How long do we stay?"

"A week. If they ain't no sign of them, no fire or nothin' by the end o' that time, we'll be durn sure they're done fer!"

"It won't take a week," thought the Lone Ranger. Hunger already asserted itself strongly. He and Tonto had been too busy to stop for food, and he knew there was none on the island. Thirst would be another enemy. The only available water, was this rank stuff through which they waded, and it would be contaminated without question.

Even if they made the island safely, camping without a fire at night to keep away the stinging insects, would be torture.

He could hear the lawmen moving about, following their leader's commands as they placed themselves at intervals around the bog. For the time at least, the Sheriff planned a waiting game. The Lone Ranger and Tonto moved ahead once more.

The Lone Ranger had long since discarded the idea of going directly to the Sheriff with the entire story. It was too fantastic to be believed. In addition to the looted safe, and the gunfire, a score of witnesses had seen them race from the express office and each witness would be glad to add they'd carried the gold with them as they fled. Imagination would make them certain of it.

Finally, dripping slime, the Lone Ranger and Tonto reached the island. It was a small place, grown high with grass, and spotted with the fallen trunks of ancient trees, now rotted and eaten by worms. Here and there, the masked man saw places where buried treasure had been sought in vain. The air was sticky, humid, and the heat oppressive, but the ground was firm and dry and he sank to it, almost overcome by sheer exhaustion. Tonto squatted at his side, his face drawn and tired-looking.

"Mebbe" suggested the Indian, "we make escape, after dark."

"That's what they'll be expecting us to do, Tonto. They'll be looking for that." He pulled off his high boots, and spilled water from them, then put them in the sun to dry. Tonto in turn, slipped off his moccasins and followed suit.

"Sheriff Potter is smarter than I thought."

Tonto nodded slowly without speaking.

"And determined. If he waits a week, and we don't come out and surrender, he will wait longer. Then he won't leave, before he or some of his men have done their best to explore the bog."

"That right," agreed the Indian who understood the nature of the Sheriff fully as well as the masked man.

He waited calmly, knowing the active mind of the Lone Ranger was trying to devise some means of out-witting the law, for the time being, so they might es-cape to be free and help the law, later on.

Many times Tonto had followed the Lone Ranger into peril of almost every sort. Even now, while men with guns were surrounding the swamp, prepared to shoot to kill on sight, he still held to his confidence in the Lone Ranger.

Removing his bandanna, the masked man wiped away the blotches of greenish scum that had spattered his face and mask. This done, he gave his attention to the two ivory-handled weapons. The working parts, protected as they had been by the holsters, were quite dry. For a time he studied them, then jammed one back in leather. The other he broke, spilling the cartridges in the palm of his hand. Those cartridges were made of solid silver!

Many times, the silver bullets had identified the Lone Ranger. People tried to trace him, by trying to learn where they were made, but they were never successful. Tonto alone knew where and how those silver slugs were cast, and the masked man's secret was quite safe with Tonto.

The Indian watched his friend. Saw him contemplate the weights as they lay on the palm of his hand. Silently then, Tonto drew a lead-filled cartridge from his belt. There were five others to match it, and he held the load out for the Lone Ranger. He knew the masked man's thoughts. He was considering whether or not to make a break for it, race shooting, toward his horse and hope that by dropping one or two of the lawmen, he might get away. Tonto knew that when, if ever, one of the Lone Ranger's guns snuffed out a human life, it would not be done with a bullet of silver. He had never killed. Even when facing the lowest type of craven outlaw, he shot to wound. In this last extremity, would he be justified?

The Lone Ranger made his decision. Slowly, deliberately, he reloaded the gun. Not with the bullets held by Tonto. He replaced the cartridges of silver.

"I have an idea, Tonto," he said softly. "We won't give up yet. Neither will we stay here to starve. We'll get what rest we can, between now and sundown and hope our horses, too, can rest. Then, at sundown—." He didn't finish. Tonto understood the rest. He had a plan, but whatever that plan was, it didn't involve murder.

He stretched his length on the grass, putting his bandanna over his face to give some protection against insects. Then the Sheriff's voice came to him. It was sharp and clear. "Masked man!" came the shout, "we know yer in there an' sooner or later we'll get yuh. We got enough on you, tuh hang yuh, but yer entitled to a fair trial by jury." The Sheriff paused, and then went on, "You an' the redskin come out holdin' yer hands high, an' you'll get a square deal."

Tonto looked somewhat amused. The last thing he could expect from the Lone Ranger, was surrender to the lawmen.

The masked man gave no reply to the Sheriff. To Tonto, he said, "He may be bluffing. We'll not answer."

"Yuh hear me," bellowed Sheriff Potter. "Come out an' git a fair trial, or stay there an' rot. We got the place surrounded."

"Perhaps the Sheriff will have trouble keeping some of the more superstitious deputies here after dark." There was a half smile on the Lone Ranger's mouth as he spoke through the bandanna.

"If you don't come out," the Sheriff spoke again, "we aim tuh come an' get yuh."

"Not just yet," murmured the Lone Ranger. "Not until our horses have a chance to rest. They'll need strength for the plan I have in mind."

"What do-um?"

"Wait, Tonto. Wait till sundown. Wait till the fog begins to rise, and in the meantime, rest." In a few more moments, the Lone Ranger slept. Surrounded on all sides by men who sought to kill him, he depended on his judgement and understanding of men to protect him. He felt confident that no attempt to penetrate the bog would be made before sundown. He felt equally sure that age-old superstitions about the Devil's Bog would force the sheriff to take a decisive step before dark rather than argue with his men to keep them there all night.

Tonto, following the lead of his master, sprawled his length and dozed, ready to waken instantly at the softest sound of anyone approaching through the swamp.

CHAPTER VIII

"The Escape."

The afternoon seemed endless to the deputies and even longer to Sheriff Potter. The grizzled old lawman spent his time going from one man to the other. Each had growls of complaint for him.

"Sittin' waitin' like this, is drivin' me loco," was Hank Hawkin's grumble. Slim Purdy "vowed" he'd "never seen mosquiters as big as these uns," and he showed a dozen welts on his hands and face. He spent most of his time slapping at the insects, and the rest of his time cursing them.

Potter gave Slim a few words of encouragement, and told of the standing reward for the capture of Express robbers, then moved on thirty yards to where Tim Frawley squatted on the plain beside the bog. "Hain't goin' tuh stay here after dark," promised Tim. "Man an' boy I've listened tuh the stories o' what goes on in this place fer forty-odd years, an' I don't hanker tuh be close by when it ain't daylight."

Several of the others voiced the same determination.

Potter himself, was apprehensive of the Devil's Bog, but in his eagerness to capture the masked man and the Indian alive, he put all fear and trepidation aside. He knew, though, that something would have to be done before dark, or his men, many of them, would desert the manhunt.

"We won't be here after dark," he promised Tim. "I figger on givin' them two one more chance tuh come out, an' if they don't come, we'll draw straws an' two men will go in after 'em."

"I'd sooner," replied Tim, "go in an' try tuh git them two, then stay here after dark. Only we don't know that they're alive."

"I marked the place they entered the swamp. If it ain't quicksand, we'll keep goin' fer the island. If it IS quicksand, we'll know them two are done fer."

"Why not try smokin' 'em out, Sheriff? I know a time when we had a couple crooks holed up in a cave, an' they wouldn't come out. We hung around there all day, an' every time a man went near the cave, a bullet clipped his whiskers. Then we built a fire so's the wind could carry the smoke tuh the cave, an' them two come out pronto, holdin' their hands high."

"That's all right, if they's any wind tuh move that smoke, Tim, but you c'n see from yer pipe that the smoke goes straight up without a breath of a breeze tuh carry it where it'd do some good."

"That's so, Sheriff. I never'd have thought of that."

"Fact is, if they jest got a whiff of that pipe, it'd be enough tuh fetch 'em out . . . or choke 'em."

Tim looked hurt, and Sheriff Potter moved away. He returned to the tethered horses, and examined the captured white stallion and the paint horse with a critical eye. They were powerful animals, finer than any he'd ever seen. He tried to make friends with the white horse, but finally gave up with a growl about a "doggone one-man hoss." In midafternoon, he shouted once more into the fastness of the bog, and as before, got no reply. He circled the bog again, pausing for a few words with each of his men, and finally, near sunset, called them in together.

"I got here, a handful o' straws," he said. "One of 'em is short, an' the rest are long. I'm passin' 'em around an' each of you men take one. The crittur that draws the short one, goes with me. Is that clear?"

"Goes where?"

The Sheriff pointed, and the men, without exception, frowned, and hesitated.

"What's the matter? Have I got a bunch of mangy, yaller-livered Digger Injuns here, or have I got a body o' white men, swore tuh uphold law an' order, an' capture killers?"

Several of the men shifted their weight uneasily from one foot to the other, and glanced at the ground.

"T'ain't me," murmured one, "I got a wife an' young un tuh think of though."

"Draw straws," commanded the Sheriff. He held his closed fist, with the straws poking out above it, toward the man who stood nearest. After some deliberation, the deputy closed his eyes, and drew. He looked at his choice, and his face lighted. Another drew, and then the rest.

Intent on what they believed to be a selection of one to die, none of the lawmen noticed the faintest of lapping sounds. Had they glanced toward the horses, they might have seen the white one cock his ears in attention, or a shrewd observer might have thought the tense, alert attitude of the horse a little strange, but each man was concerned with drawing straws.

The Lone Ranger was in water to his thighs a second time. He made scarcely a sound as he moved closer to the shore, bending tall reeds and breaking down the grass to mark his path. At the bank, he listened, till he learned that none had noticed him, and then made his slow way back toward the island.

Jack Walton drew the short straw, much to the relief of all the others. He nodded slowly, and told the Sheriff he was ready to go into the swamp. "Don't you coyotes start offerin' yer sympathies," he growled, "because we're comin' out of there alive, an' totin' them two outlaws with us. When the time comes tuh whack up the reward money, I'll have the laugh on all of yuh."

He inspected his guns, took off excess clothing, jerked his hat down tight, and was ready.

The others, standing close to the horses, gave much in the way of advice, until the Sheriff ordered them back to their posts, in case the fugitives tried to escape in another direction.

The sun was gone, and fog rose from the swale. It would soon be dense, as the air grew cooler. Sheriff Potter with a gun in each hand, led the way, Jack Walton close behind him.

"Right about here is where he went in," the leader said. "If he found ground fer walkin' on beneath that water, we'll find it to."

They splashed at first, and then acquired the knack of moving through the water with almost no sound, by sliding their feet along the bottom, instead of lifting them.

"Curious," muttered Sheriff Potter, "how the path is marked out so clear. This won't be no trouble at all."

"I'm sinkin' tuh my ankles," growled Jack Walton.

"Sure, but it's mud, an' not quicksand. Them two had this trail all marked out. The critters knowed they'd be able tuh reach that island safe an' sound."

"They'll hear us, in spite of how careful we are."

"All right. Let 'em hear us. It'll be a six-gun show-down anyhow. The sooner they open fire an' show themselves, the sooner we'll be able tuh finish up this job."

Confident now that they had little to fear from quicksand, and certain the men they wanted were ahead, the Sheriff and his deputy plunged on.

A scant ten yards separated them from the island, when it happened. A strong arm grabbed the Sheriff from the side, and a brown hand clamped across his mouth to stifle the exclamation of surprise. He tried to turn, or bring his guns to bear, but a rope jerked tight and pinioned his arms to his sides.

Jack Walton, close behind, saw the Indian who reached from close beside the path. He tried to shout a warning, but found himself in a predicament similar to the Sheriff's. The Lone Ranger had no difficulty keeping Walton quiet. While one arm circled the deputy's neck, the hand clamping the mouth, he used his other hand to draw the rope tight.

So carefully planned was the Lone Ranger's scheme, that both he and Tonto arched lassos through the air at the same instant. Neither rope was noticed, until too late. Neither of the captured men realized that a rope was used, until they felt it drawn tight, while strong hands shut off all speech.

Then, still keeping their prisoners silent, the masked

man and Tonto dragged them to the island. There they finished the job of roping, and added gags. Sheriff Potter glared balefully at his captors, and his eyes promised vengeance. The Lone Ranger knew that in his present angry mood, there was no use trying to give the Sheriff explanations. Instead, he said, "Your men will find you, and if they don't, you'll be able to free yourself in half an hour or so. We're going to leave you here, unhurt. I hope the next time we meet, you'll have proof that we're not the men you want."

Potter squirmed frantically, but the ropes were strong, and the knots well tied.

"Now then, Tonto, we're ready."

Tonto nodded, and moved to the water's edge. The Lone Ranger drew one of his guns, and pressed it hard against the Indian's back, while Tonto raised his hands high overhead. In this fashion, the two went once more through the vile-smelling water, toward the mainland.

Tim Frawley saw two figures coming through the fog. The first one, he saw, was an Indian who held his hands up in surrender.

"Boys," yelled Tim, "hyar they come. That didn't take 'em long. Come on, boys, we're takin' 'em back alive."

The rest of the men shouted their delight, and

abandoning their posts, came running to meet the prisoners and captors.

"Where's the other one?" yelled Tim.

He squinted through the rising fog, trying to discern whether Sheriff Potter or Jack Walton brought the Indian in. He saw the man with the gun, gesture over his shoulder.

"Comin' right out?" cried Tim. He didn't wait for the answer, but went on to meet the couple.

The Lone Ranger and Tonto faced the most crucial moment in their entire plan. They were on the mainland, with just a few yards of fog separating them from the band of lawmen. They couldn't go much further without the ruse being known.

"Steady now," the masked man whispered to his friend. "Do you see the horses?" He saw Tonto's head nod slightly.

Then a yell of dismay rang from Slim. "That ain't Jack Walton, that's the masked man!"

The cry was echoed by a dozen others, and was the signal for fast action. Tonto's hands dropped to his sides, his head lowered, and he raced along the ground.

The Lone Ranger, hesitating only long enough to give a shout, ran after him. The shout brought a whinny of pleasure from the white horse.

"Come on, Silver, old boy!" cried the Lone Ranger

again, and a frantic pounding of hoofs accompanied by angry snorts and bellows told how Silver struggled with the tether.

The lawmen recovered from surprise, snatched their guns, and started firing. Their aim was uncertain, hurried. The fog made aiming hard, and the way both runners crouched and dodged, made it even harder. Bullets whined close to Tonto and one pierced the masked man's hat, before they reached the horses.

Tonto's hand came up from his belt holding a gleaming knife. It lashed down, cutting Silver loose. Then up, and down again, the keen blade slashing through the rope that held the paint horse.

"Don't shoot our hosses," screamed one of the lawmen. "Nemmine the hosses," cried another, "Drop them two hombres." But their chance was gone. Without touching a stirrup, the Lone Ranger leaped to the saddle. Even before his feet found the stirrups, Silver lunged ahead, anticipating the masked man's familiar cry of "Hi-Yo Silver, Away-y-y."

The cry rang out a second time, but as far as the astonished lawmen were concerned, the Lone Ranger and Tonto, mistaken for thieves and murderers, were gone. Gone into the increasing fog on their rested horses. Gone to find the outlaws, for whom they'd been mistaken.

CHAPTER IX

"Sanctuary."

The half day of rest had given new life to the strong muscles of Silver and Scout. The horses seemed to sense the peril of their masters, and raced on across the plains with their old, familiar speed. Silver, more powerful than Tonto's horse, held back slightly so the Indian could keep abreast. For some time, the wind lashing at their faces, the Lone Ranger and Tonto rode without exchanging words.

As darkness came, a breeze sprang up, and scudding clouds blew across the sky, obscuring the moon from time to time. Distant lightning flared, and a faint rumble of thunder sounded over the rhythm of the hoofbeats.

They headed northwest, where the Lone Ranger and Tonto had a cache of food in a patch of Douglas fir. They had to travel light, and frequently when overstocked with food, they set aside unperishable things, especially that which was in tins, and marked the place. This was only one of many occasions when

64

their forethought might prove to be the difference between starvation, and food.

Were it not for the cache, the nearest source of supply would be Black River, where they dared not risk capture by trying to buy food. Any other community would mean at least another day and night of riding before it was reached.

True, both men were skilled hunters, and Tonto could fashion a spear or hook to catch some fish, but all these means of getting food took time, and time was one thing that was too precious to be wasted. Furthermore they couldn't hunt at night.

The wind freshened and packed the clouds in a denser mass while new storm clouds pushed up from the horizon. The Lone Ranger caught Tonto's eye, and shouted, "Rain?"

The Indian shouted back to make himself heard above the thunder of the hoofs, and the more frequent, and louder thunder overhead, "Rain come plenty soon."

The masked man was glad. He and Tonto would be soaked before they reached the shelter of the firs, but good cleansing rain would be welcome to wash away the filth of the bog that still clung to their clothing.

Rain would also wash away the hoofprints.

With rested horses, the hoofprints weren't the hazard they'd been that morning, but they still would give the Sheriff a clue as to which direction the fugitives had taken. The Lone Ranger had no illusions about Sheriff Potter. He knew the lawman would pursue them and continue in pursuit until the trail's end. He had to evade the posse in one way or another until he'd found the stolen gold, the ones who stole it, and the killers of Ben Jenkins.

He realized the lack of clues. It seemed an almost hopeless task to find the men he sought. What clues there were, if any, were south in Black River, perhaps in that express office. That at least, would have to be his ultimate starting point in the hunt.

A jagged streak of lightning dropped close by, and the white flash lighted the prairie for miles ahead. Almost instantly the thunder exploded in a way that left no doubt about the rain. In fact, the first drops fell almost with the thunder. Large, heavy drops, that hurt when the speed of the Lone Ranger made them slap against his face.

But even though the water stung, he welcomed it. Then the downpour came, with lightning more frequently showing the plain ahead. Still there was no break in the steady pounding of the hoofs. The horses seemed to like the rain. They put forth even more speed. In a little while, there were puddles on the ground. Puddles that would certainly melt away all hoofprints. The Lone Ranger could see them when the lightning flared, and hear them, as the pounding hoofs splashed through them.

Mud, he knew, would bespatter horses and riders, but this gave him no concern. Mud, good prairie mud, was clean after the vile muck of the bog.

For the first time in twenty hours, the Lone Ranger felt genuine hope of escape. For the first time since his flight from the express office, he drew a breath that wasn't tainted with fear. Not fear of capture or of death. It was fear of failure in his self-appointed mission. A dread of capture because with capture would come the doom of any chance to find the killers, a dread that with his capture and hanging, the robbery of the express office and the murder of Ben Jenkins, would be marked closed.

It was late at night when the two arrived at the woods. They skirted the fringe of trees, while Tonto watched for a familiar sign that would mark the cache. In the darkness, it would be easy to miss the huge boulder, so both horses were slowed to a walk. A flash of lightning showed the rock a little way ahead, just inside the outermost trees of the wooded area.

In the shelter of the firs, the rain was scarcely more than a drizzle.

The Lone Ranger dismounted and stood beside the Indian. He waited, while Tonto paced off a certain number of steps in a direction determined as much by instinct as by any other means. Tonto paused, and crouched at the base of a tall monarch of the forest. Here he found a thicket of stunted growth, and reached his arm in.

When Tonto called, the masked man went to join him. "Have you found it?"

Tonto said, "Tonto find-um. Here all food. Here cache."

The darkness was intense but the Lone Ranger could hear the clink of cans, the rustle of tarpaulin, and other sounds that Tonto made as he brought necessities from their hiding place.

"We'll camp right here for the night," decided the Lone Ranger. "I think we can risk a fire."

"Make small fire," agreed the Indian. "Tonto fix-um shelter. You fix um fire."

Each of the men carried a small hand axe as one of the indispensable parts of their equipment. For some strange reason, the Sheriff hadn't bothered to unpack the duffle from the horses while he had them.

The lightning, when it came, which was less often than before, gave enough light in the woods for the Lone Ranger to spot a fallen tree. Walking on a thick carpet of fallen fir-needles, he went unerringly to the tree and began to cut dry wood from the underside.

Meanwhile, Tonto had taken advantage of the instant flashes of light, to locate the branches he would use for a shelter. His own axe rose and fell as he lopped off broad, low branches of evergreen and stacked them in a pile beside the cache.

When he had a sufficient supply, working almost entirely by the sense of touch, he trimmed one branch clean and fashioned a pole about eight feet in length. He braced this between low forks of trees spaced about six feet apart. From this horizontal beam, some four feet off the ground, he slanted other poles, and then across the slanting stringers of the lean-to, spread the branches.

By the time he finished, the Lone Ranger had a small fire going at the open side of the shelter. It gave enough light for the Indian to add the finishing touches to his handicraft. He made a soft pad of smaller branches on the floor of the lean-to, and over these spread the tarpaulin, and atop the canvas, the dry blankets it had protected.

The fire lighted the inside of the shelter with a warm glow. The shelter itself would serve to conceal the fire from one side, and the dense woods beyond, from the other.

While the masked man added more wood to a supply to maintain the fire throughout the night, Tonto located small stones, and placed them in such a way that they would balance frying pan and coffee pot.

He filled the pot from a spring near the big rock that served as a landmark, and put it close to the fire to boil. His knife opened several of the tin cans, and when the Lone Ranger came to join him, with the last armload of wood, the appetizing odor of sizzling bacon, bubbling coffee, and fresh baking filled the lean-to.

Tonto had his own special recipe for what he called "Twist." It was a satisfying form of biscuit, which was cooked by rolling the dough into a thin length of about ten inches, then spiralling it around a green-wood stick from which the bark had been peeled. Several sticks held their bread close to the fire, to bake.

Bread, bacon, good water, and coffee, unsweetened. It was hardly a meal for an epicure but to the two half-starved men, eaten in the warmth and shelter of the lean-to, while they squatted on the comfortable woolen blankets, padded by the evergreen whose fragrance spiced the food, it tasted far better than many a royal meal, served with all the pomp of a monarch's court.

Even the horses were provided for by the cache. After many days of scant grazing, the oats, made into a sort of warm mash by the addition of hot water and salt, were good.

What the food lacked in variety, it made up in quantity, and both men ate their fill. Tired to the point of exhaustion, it was a temptation to roll into the blankets at once, but there were certain chores that it was not their habit to postpone. The Lone Ranger saw that the horses were made comfortable for the night, while Tonto washed the few utensils. Saddles were suspended safe above the ground, and the fire well-banked, so a new breeze springing up couldn't blow sparks where they would start a forest fire. Both men turned in then, and almost instantly, were sound asleep.

CHAPTER X

"JACK BANNERMAN."

When the Lone Ranger wakened in the morning, he found that Tonto was up ahead of him, and gone from the fragrant evergreen lean-to. The realization that his friend was missing, startled the mystery rider momentarily, but common sense told him that he would have wakened or been wakened by the alarm of the horses, had anything out of the ordinary happened during the night.

The fire had been rekindled and utensils for the morning meal laid out in readiness. Through the trees, the masked man caught the reflection of the slanting rays of the morning sun on a swift-running stream. Then he saw Tonto. The Indian, with an improvised net, knelt beside the water, trying to trap some fish for breakfast.

It was barely later than sunrise. Not yet time to saddle the horses and start out on the next dangerous step of his mission of justice. It was comfortable there in the shelter, and there was a lot of thinking and planning to be done. For just a few moments, he decided, he would remain beneath the blanket, and consider his plans for the day.

He knew he had to return to Black River. There, if anywhere, would be found the solution to the mysterious murder of Ben Jenkins, the theft of the gold, and also the lesser mystery that puzzled him. The scream and shot from the express office.

Today was the second day of the three-day celebration in town. Perhaps, in the crowds, he would go unnoticed, especially if he went un-masked. No one had had a close look at him. If his clothes didn't betray him, he might go undiscovered. He'd change clothes, for others he carried in his sougan . . . go into town as a rancher or a cowboy. He would remove the mask, but his real face would be covered with a disguise.

The criminals in town, he felt, would be secure in their belief that the law already accused him and Tonto of the robberies. That as long as the Sheriff's posse hadn't found his new refuge, they would be able to remain in town, secure even from suspicion.

The masked man tossed aside the blanket, rose, and stretched his full height. Dipping water from the pail, he took a long refreshing drink, and went to the stream to join Tonto.

The Indian had already netted two fish of moderate

size, and was ready to return to camp. "I'll be with you, Tonto, as soon as I've washed," the Lone Ranger told his friend.

Tonto nodded, and left the stream. By the time the Lone Ranger arrived, the fish were already cleaned, and frying. While they cooked, he prepared for his venture. The preparations were strange, and showed the extent to which the Lone Ranger had gone in perfecting the details of disguise in his crusade against the lawlessness of the west.

He set aside the high-heeled boots worn by all horsemen in the early west, and in their place, pulled on boots which had practically no heels at all. This made him appear shorter. His fawn-colored shirt and black neckerchief gave way to the more gaudy attire affected by the cowboys in town on one of their infrequent sprees. Bibless overalls, tucked in the high boots, replaced the familiar trousers of dark color.

Then, propping a small mirror on a convenient log, the Lone Ranger gave careful attention to his face. He removed the mask, and opened a small tin box. False hair, and balsam gum to hold it in place soon provided sideburns, and a neat mustache. He rubbed stain in his hair to make it match the mustache and blend perfectly into the sideburns. He made his brows a little shaggy, and then opened a small vial. The stuff he poured into the palms of his hands, was

a stain that Tonto prepared from the roots of certain trees. Rubbing his palms together briskly, the Lone Ranger smeared the stain over his face and neck, and worked it carefully into the crevices of his ears. His skin took on a darker tone, and yet a perfectly natural one for a dark-haired man who spent all his time out of doors.

He took a lot more care than usual in his preparations. A hurried disguise would suffice in most cases, even as far as Sheriff Potter was concerned, but Jack Bannerman was shrewd. While the manager of the express office hadn't seen the masked man previously, he was shrewd enough to recognize that a disguise was worn, and this would be enough to arouse his suspicions. He held his job with the express people because of his careful attention to details, and the Lone Ranger, knowing him from reputation, had the utmost respect for his cleverness. It was frequently said that Bannerman could size a man up with a glance, and that with an hour's conversation, he could tell almost to a certainty, what the future held for that man. "Yes," the Lone Ranger murmured, at the end of his thoughts of Bannerman. "I'll have to be mighty careful, because Bannerman is ONE man that I want to talk to in Black River."

He finished his preparations, by pulling on a goat-skin vest, and a floppy, inexpensive black felt hat that was somewhat the worse for wear, and badly wrinkled from being wrapped in a sougan. Then he joined Tonto at the fire.

"You look-um like new man," muttered the Indian.

The Lone Ranger half smiled at the approval of his disguise. Tonto forked one of the crisp brown fish to a tin plate and passed it to him. While they ate, the Lone Ranger outlined the result of all his planning, and instructed Tonto in the part that he must play.

Tonto frowned in disapproval. "You take-um all risk."

"I know, Tonto, but this is my job! You can't handle it, because you would be too easily recognized. You'll have to keep in the background for a time, and let me go ahead."

"Um." It was agreement, but with reservations. "Plenty risk," he added.

"I don't think so. After the escape from the Devil's Bog, I begin to think we lead a charmed life. We wouldn't have been permitted to escape from there, if Fate intended us to fail in our purpose."

While they ate, the Lone Ranger told Tonto what to do about moving the camp to a place nearer town. Once more, Tonto tried to persuade the mystery rider to allow him to go with him to Black River. "No," replied the white man. "There will be far less risk, if I go there alone. Besides, you'll have to watch your

chance to move our camp while I am gone. Mark
the new camp in the usual way, and I will find it."
A short time later, the Lone Ranger rode off, and
Tonto was alone.

In his stocking feet, Jack Bannerman was six feet
two inches tall. His high-heeled boots added another
couple inches, so when he stood beside his desk in
the express office, he towered over Sheriff Potter.
Bannerman's iron-gray hair seemed to fairly bristle,
and his short-clipped mustache quivered as he spoke;
a sure sign that his rage and fury were almost out
of hand.

"You," he roared at the Sheriff, "you come tuh this
office an' tell me them two got away! You had 'em
clear surrounded in that bog, an' STILL they got
away!"

Sheriff Potter did his best to remain cool. "I tell
you, Bannerman," he said for the tenth time, "there
ain't a man alive would have figured them two tuh
pull a trick like what they done."

It was the morning of the second of the three holidays in Black River. Potter and his men, after a futile
search in the rain of the night before, had ridden in
drenched to the skin, cold, and hungry. The lawman
had no intention of abandoning the search. He had
returned only to equip himself and his men for a fresh
start. Bannerman, the iron-jawed jack, was the only

man who could talk to Potter as he was doing. Potter understood big Jack and liked him.

He knew that the sooner Bannerman talked his rage out of his system, the sooner he'd cool off.

"I tell yuh, Potter, school kids could have held him there, school kids mind yuh, an' waited till he starved tuh death, or surrendered, but YOU couldn't do it. No, YOU couldn't trap him. You an' that pack of slow-witted, dumb-thinkin' mavericks yuh call deputies had tur try an' be smart an' go in after him. Yuh had to go an' do the very thing he figgered you tuh do, an' give him the chance tuh git away." He paused for breath.

Sheriff Potter wouldn't have taken that from any other man alive. He was a good Sheriff, and he knew it, just as he knew that Bannerman would regret most of the hard things he was saying, when he thought them over. He stood there, half smiling.

"Well, blast yuh, say somethin'!" Bannerman shouted. "What're yuh standin' there for? What're yuh in town for anyhow? Why ain't yuh out ridin' his trail, bringin' him back here? Yuh don't expect tuh find him in Black River do yuh?"

"Nope."

"Then go where you can find him. Him an' that Indian rode hosses, an' hosses make tracks. GIT GOIN'!"

"Hosses make tracks, sure enough Jack," said the Sheriff softly. "They make tracks in mud, an' rain washes them same tracks away. That same rain soaks men tuh the skin, an' when a man is wet tuh the skin an' without grub, an' out of smokin' an' chewin' tobacco, he sure ain't much interested in ridin' all over Hell's half acre hopin' tuh run across them tracks he's lost by accident."

"I suppose you'll stay here now, till the celebration's over! Well, let me tell you . . . " the accusing forefinger came into use again, "you nor none of your men get a single drink in town until that thief is brought in!"

"We just come tuh town long enough tuh get some grub, dry clothes an' things, an' then we're ridin' out again."

"You better."

"And now, Bannerman, throw a halter on that line of talk an' calm down enough so a man can get some sensible words out of yuh."

Bannerman flopped to his chair, sunk his teeth almost savagely in a plug of black, molasses-flavored tobacco and bit off a chunk. "All right," he snapped, "let's hear some sensible words!"

"Night before last," began the Sheriff, "the thing that brought us all here on the run, was the sound of a shot an' a scream."

"I know."

"The redskin held us off for a time, till he an' the white man could make their get-away. We took up the chase as soon as we could, and didn't spend time lookin' around here."

"I heard that you'd might just as well have looked around. Got off on the wrong trail, didn't yuh?" Bannerman seemed to delight in pointing out the Sheriff's mistakes.

"We got off on the wrong trail, but we blamed soon found the right one. Now the point is, I didn't wait here to see who it was that screamed, or who that shot was fired at. I took a look around this office, just long enough to see that the safe was looted, and the gold gone. There wasn't any dead man here, or no sign of a wounded man."

"There was a dead man all right. A GOOD man, too."

"Who?"

"Dick Tuttle."

"Tuttle! The kid that worked in here?"

"The same!" Bannerman spoke more softly.

"Where was he found?

"Out in back. Poor kid, he was so darn ambitious! He wanted to learn all there was to know about this business. He always talked about the things he was goin' to do when he owned an express company of his own. Talked about the things he'd do with important money, when he had it. Hours meant nothin' to him. He worked night an' day, to do a good job here, and now ... " Bannerman hesitated after his eulogy, "he's gone."

"Found out in back you say?"

The manager of the office nodded. The hard lines of his grizzled face softened. He had thought more of Tuttle than he cared to admit. "The gold," he said, "is gone. It's a big loss, an' it won't do the reputation of the town or me any good to have that report go out, but there's more gold. Dick Tuttle can't be replaced."

"Who found his remains?"

"Couple of his friends. Vinton and Brady. They thought it was him they heard screamin'."

"How'd they come to find him?"

"It seems," explained Jack Bannerman, "that they were all celebratin' when Tuttle thought he saw dark forms movin' about here. The other two tried to tell him he was seein' things, but he had tuh be sure. That's how interested he was in the job here. He left 'em, an' come to investigate. Then the next they heard was the scream and the shot, and after you an' your men left, they hunted around till they found Dick's body a hundred feet from the back door."

"Carried there?"

"Nope. It seems he was hit bad, but must've

thought he could get to my house and wake me up. He likely tried to do that. They buried him yesterday morning."

"Yep. Brady an' Vinton was his closest friends, an' bein' as he had no family, they sort of took charge. He left a sort of will, leavin' what he owned to them."

"I see."

"Figgered it best to hold the last rites right away, before the folks got to celebratin' too much on Frontier Day."

Sheriff Potter thought for a moment, and then asked, "He lived with Vinton an' Brady, didn't he?"

"That's right, Sheriff."

"Don't seem to me anyone would be in much condition for a funeral, after the way they'd been carryin' on all night."

"Wasn't many there."

"Now let me get some facts straight. Brady done some work in this office too, didn't he?"

Bannerman nodded slowly.

What about Vinton?"

"Tuttle an' Brady wanted me to hire Vinton, but I got old Ben Jenkins on the payroll, an' can't hire anymore men right now."

"Where is Ben Jenkins?"

"I don't know, Sheriff. Fact is, I ain't seen him since day before yesterday."

The Sheriff thought deeply. He would have liked to have been in attendance at the burial of Dick Tuttle. He knew the Black River doctor, the coroner, and most of the others who were generally involved in sudden death and burial, and knew that since the eve of the celebration they'd all been imbibing freely from the many bars in town. If it weren't for the serious nature of the murder, and the likeable personality of the murder victim, thought of the services would have been amusing.

Of course, neither Bannerman, nor Potter, knew that old Ben Jenkins too, was killed, and that his burial had been a sincere and simple one conducted by the Lone Ranger at the edge of Devil's Bog.

CHAPTER XI

"THE LONE RANGER ARRIVES."

If Cal Caswell had started for the Frontier Day blowout one day sooner, or if it hadn't rained the night before, there would perhaps have been many days more elapsed, before Sheriff Potter, Jack Bannerman, and the others of Black River learned of Ben Jenkins' death. As it happened, however, Cal Caswell had to pass the Devil's Bog on his way to Black River, and having gotten a late start from his ranch, it was noon when he arrived in town. As Sheriff Potter was about to leave Bannerman's office, Caswell rode up with his horse blowing white specks of lather.

He whooped to Bannerman to come out and hear "The most gosh-awful news a man ever rid tuh tell!"

Bannerman knew Cal and his reputation for making mountains out of gopher hills and paid scant attention. Sheriff Potter, however, sensed that this time Caswell really brought astounding news. "What's all the rumpus?" he demanded.

"It's about Ben Jenkins."

"What about him?" asked Bannerman impatiently. Caswell paused to catch his breath, and then went on to explain. "I was headin' here, ridin' hard through the slop an' mud o' last night's rain. I come past the Devil's Bog a short while after daybreak. What do I see?"

"The bog," guessed Sheriff Potter.

"More'n that."

"Well, go on an' tell it," snapped Jack Bannerman. "We ain't playin' guessin' games."

"I seen a puddle o' water on the ground, lookin' tuh be about six foot long an' two foot wide. What's that remind yuh of?"

"Talk, blast yuh," roared Bannerman impatiently, "an' stop askin' questions."

"A grave, ain't that so? Well, sir, it reminded me of a grave that's new dug an' filled, an' the loose mud settled some from water. I was outright curious. Jest enough so, tuh sort of stop an' dig a little. First thing I knowed, I'd struck a body. I dug deeper, workin' like all git out." As Cal warmed to his subject, he waved his arms, and raised his voice dramatically. "There I was, diggin' away like a woodchuck, an' I didn't stop, not even tuh get a breath, till I'd found that it was the body of Ben Jenkins. All wrapped in a blanket!"

Both Bannerman and the Sheriff fired questions at

Caswell, until they were convinced he told the truth, and then hammered for more information, which they finally got in Caswell's provoking, question-asking style.

He told them all the gruesome details; of the wound, the apparent submersion in quicksand, and the loading of the body on his horse. "I left it," he finished, referring to the body, "in a shack outside o' town, so's not tuh git folks crowdin' 'round tuh see what's what."

"Good judgement," the Sheriff approved. He looked at Bannerman, anticipating the usual outburst, and cutting criticism about himself for not finding Ben when he was there the previous day. Instead he saw the man's face, actually pale. Bannerman's lips were compressed into a thin line, and his big hands clenched hard, until the knuckles whitened.

"Potter," said the manager of the office in a low, crackling manner, "That settles it. The loss of two of my men, gives me the right tuh throw in with you on this manhunt. From now on, this gol-blasted office can run itself, or struggle along with Vinton. I'm joinin' tuh run down this masked man an' redskin. Come on an' swear me in as a deputy."

The two strong men faced each other. Cal Caswell left to spread his news over all the bars in town, and make up for the time lost in celebrating the Frontier Day.

The few men who were in the bars at noon, looked sorry that they'd not slept off the effects of the night before and all its revelry. The afternoon's games and contests would be well attended, but until then, there was little action, and nothing to warrant getting out of warm beds, and hanging around the town, just waiting.

The sky was still heavily overcast, and the air was raw and chilly, with a constant threat of more rain. While Bannerman and Potter discussed their plans, and waited for the possemen to get into dry clothing and pack their saddle bags with food, they sat next to the fly-specked window of the Busy Bee Restaurant, drinking black coffee.

It was then, that another new arrival rode down the street. The stranger was tall, and broad-shouldered, but his nondescript attire made him practically inconspicuous despite his size. The battered black hat he wore, indicated that recent financial difficulties might have brought about a swap that gave him that old hat and a sum of cash, for the style of hat that every cowboy takes such pride in owning.

The horse the stranger rode was so spattered with mud that its original color was practically obscured. The slow gait of the stallion gave no indication of the great muscles of steel that gave it lightning-like speed, and none would have guessed that the dejected manner in which the horse's head drooped, and the ears fell back, was the result of painstaking training on the part of the man in the saddle.

The man wore the manner of a cowboy in town for Frontier Day, hoping to see and enjoy what takes place, and perhaps win a contest or two that carried cash prizes, but with scarcely the price of a meal in his pocket. A man who came to watch, but not indulge.

It was in this disguise that Bannerman and Potter, unsuspectingly of course, saw the Lone Ranger come to town.

CHAPTER XII

"Suspected."

The strong, black coffee was scalding hot, but Bannerman and Sheriff Dan Potter were content to sit and wait for it to cool. It would be half an hour or so, before the members of the posse re-assembled to continue the manhunt. Bannerman, who faced the restaurant window, idly stirred sugar in his cup while he watched the horseman across the road.

The mud-covered horse came to a slow halt. The rider seemed saddle-weary, as he swung to the ground and tossed his reins around the hitchrack. He pushed through the swinging doors of the saloon, and out of sight of the two men in the restaurant.

When the Lone Ranger entered the saloon, it took a moment for his eyes to accustom themselves to the dingy gloom of the place. A center of gaiety, brilliant with lamps in polished reflectors at night, the saloon was a drab, unhappy place in the morning. Only one bartender was on duty, to serve the half-dozen red-eyed patrons of the place.

Baldy caressed the polished mahogany bar with a damp towel while he eyed the new arrival. His handlebar mustache seemed to droop in disapproval and his calculating face expressed his thought, "Not much of a spender, he's likely here tuh watch, but not tuh buy." He deliberately turned his back to the man who leaned an elbow on the bar, and gave close attention to the high-stacked glasses of various sizes and shapes that graced the back-bar. In the mirror, the bartender could see the man who waited patiently for service. Then with something of a start, Baldy realized that while he studied the stranger's reflection, the stranger was in turn, sizing him up. The eyes of the two men met in the gaudily painted mirror; the pale, watery eyes of Baldy, and the steely, gray-blue inscrutable eyes of the Lone Ranger. The steadiness and depth of the Lone Ranger's eyes did something to Baldy. He felt his air of superiority, his confidence, drain from him. Despite the clothes and manner of the stranger, there was something—he didn't know just what it was.

"What'll it be, stranger?"

"It doesn't matter much. Give me whatever is the handiest."

Baldy squinted some at this. Men who were so careless about their liquor, usually figured on "bumming" the drink. He hesitated before reaching for a bottle. "Anything?" he asked.

The Lone Ranger had no intention of drinking the stuff so it really didn't matter to him what was served. He nodded, "Anything," and tossed a coin out.

Relieved, Baldy set out a bottle of raw liquor with a fancy label, and a glass, inviting the stranger to pour his own.

"Quiet in town, isn't it?"

"Yep. If you'd come sooner, you'd seen plenty of excitement, an' if yuh hang around long enough, you'll still see aplenty. Yer jest in between times."

"Sooner! You mean last night?"

Baldy wiped an imaginary speck from the bar. "Sure, last night an' the night before. Most of the boys sleep it off in the mornin' durin' the Frontier Day celebration."

"I see!"

Baldy turned to eye a couple of men who lingered long over their drinks at a corner table. The Lone Ranger took advantage of the moment to empty his glass into a cuspidor at his feet. When Baldy looked again, he was casually pouring himself another drink. "Anything special happen?" he asked innocently.

"Umm, had a couple of murders, an' a robbery throwed in fer good measure!"

As if hearing this news for the first time, the Lone Ranger looked up inquiringly, but Baldy seemed disinclined to go into details. The Lone Ranger understood bartenders fully as well as those who patronized the saloons frequently. He tossed another coin on the glossy bar and invited the bald-headed man to have a drink.

Baldy accepted the invitation with alacrity. "I can stand one, stranger! Ain't wet my whistle since last night." He selected the bottle for his own drink, with a lot more care than he'd shown in supplying the Lone Ranger's request, and poured himself a man-sized drink which he tossed down with a single gulp.

Baldy swallowed twice, and cleared his throat noisily. "Yes siree," he exclaimed, "that thaws a man out on a raw mornin' like this un."

"Anyone important get shot up?"

"I'd call it that! One of the boys in the express office was killed. Buried him at daybreak yesterday. Then the news came in this noon by Cal Caswell that old Ben Jenkins was murdered an' planted out near the Devil's Bog."

The Lone Ranger was doubly surprised. So Ben's body had already been found and the news of his death reported. And there HAD been a murder in the office, just before he broke through the door. Without appearing to be seeking information, he drew the entire story from the bartender. After the second drink, Baldy dropped the "stranger," and began calling the Lone Ranger "Pardner." Then it was "Pard," and by the time his recital of the grim story of murder and robbery was concluded, the stranger of a half hour previous, was being addressed as "Friend."

The Lone Ranger heard of the shooting and burial of Dick Tuttle; of the arrival of Cal Caswell with his startling story of Ben Jenkins' death, and most import-ant of all, he verified what he already suspected. That everyone in town had definitely decided that the masked man and the Indian who raced away from the Sheriff's posse were the killers and thieves.

"Cal Caswell," concluded Baldy, "will have the time o' his life tuhday. Every time he tells his story about the findin' of Ben Jenkins, the boys'll buy him a drink, an' the old galoot'll soon be roarin' drunk."

At this point, Bannerman and the Sheriff came into the saloon. They glanced at the Lone Ranger in pass-ing, and he met their gaze quite frankly. No sign of recognition showed in Dan Potter's face. The Lone Ranger's disguise had passed its first test. He followed the two men with his eyes, and saw them approach a slim man who sat alone.

"We're lookin' for you, Vinton!" Bannerman told the thin man.

"What for?" Vinton's voice was high-pitched, rasp-ing and unpleasant. He was fashionably dressed, and wore his black hair slicked back from a high forehead, and plastered down close to his head with grease. Long sideburns gave him a somewhat Latin appearance. The eyes of Vinton seemed shifty and beady, but at the distance, the Lone Ranger couldn't be sure that it was dishonesty that showed in Vinton's face.

Bannerman and the Sheriff took seats at Vinton's table without waiting to be invited. Both seemed to be on good terms with the foreign-looking man, and they treated him with a certain amount of respect, despite his obvious youth.

"Didn't Brady speak to you about that job in the office?"

Vinton shook his head slowly, to answer Bannerman's question. "Haven't seen Brady since the burial," he said. His eyes dropped to his glass and he toyed with it, making a pattern of wet rings on the table top.

"Brady'll no doubt tell you when he sees you. That job you wanted at the office is open now, if you still want it."

"Okay," muttered Vinton without enthusiasm. "I'll take it."

Bannerman looked annoyed. "If you don't want it, say so. They's aplenty of men that'd be glad of it."

"Oh, I want it all right."

"Yuh don't seem bustin' with joy about it."

"How do you expect me to feel?" Vinton showed a trace of anger, "after buryin' my friend Dick Tuttle."

Bannerman's manner softened considerably. "I expect you're hard hit by that. I can understand it. You an' Tuttle an' Brady was mighty close friends."

Vinton saddened at the man's sympathy, but to the Lone Ranger, there was a false note in the expression on the thin, high-cheek-boned face.

"Anyhow," continued Bannerman, "you see Brady, an' he'll give you the instructions. You an' he will have to take charge of things till I get back. I'm joinin' up with the Sheriff on this manhunt. I'll be back when we fetch the killers an' not before."

There was a little further conversation of no importance, and then the Sheriff and the manager of the express office left Vinton alone at the table and joined the group of men who had just ridden up, ready to start out on the trail.

Vinton remained at the table after the others left. By leaning a little sideways against the bar, the Lone Ranger could watch him, without appearing to do so. He appraised Vinton as weak-willed, but smart, in a crafty sort of way.

Baldy's voice hinted, "Another drink?"

Absently the Lone Ranger refilled his glass, and paid for it. Then when Baldy's back was turned, he quickly dumped the Three Star into the same place that the last one had gone. It was a careless gesture. He saw an expression cross Vinton's face, and then became suddenly aware that his act had been seen by Vinton, who watched his reflection in a mirror on the far side of the room.

Vinton's thin black eyebrows lifted slightly, and he tossed off the last of his drink. The thin man rose, shoved back his chair, and with something of a swagger, joined the Lone Ranger at the bar. "Set out another glass," he told the bartender. "I'm goin' to buy the stranger here, a drink!"

CHAPTER XIII

"CAPTAIN SKINNER."

Baldy now pleasantly mellow as a result of the drinks the Lone Ranger paid for, didn't notice the highly charged atmosphere—the ominous tension, that spring into existance when Vinton ordered drinks. Eager to please a couple of cash customers, the bartender slid a second whiskey glass across the bar with such precision that it stopped exactly in front of the host.

Vinton poured the drinks. First the Lone Ranger's, then his own. He ignored Baldy's expectant look, keeping his sharp, restless eyes on the tall man at his side. "You heard Bannerman tell me that I had a new job," he stated, "so I guess you don't mind joining me in a drink for good luck."

Despite the ethics and custom of the country, which the Lone Ranger understood as well as any man, he said, "I'm sorry, Vinton, but I've had about all the drinks I want."

Baldy stared in amazement at the man who re-

fused a free drink. Vinton, instead of resenting the
refusal of his hospitality, permitted a thin smile to
curve his lips. "That" he said, "is just about what I
thought." He reached for the Lone Ranger's glass,
and deliberately tilted it over the brass cuspidor near
his feet. As the fluid poured from the glass, he said.
"The cuspidor must be pretty near filled up with good
liquor by this time. Wouldn't you say so, stranger?"

"What about it?"

"It's hard for me to understand a man that drifts
into town a stranger, spends his cash for liquor to
dump into the spitoon, and buys enough drinks for
Baldy to loosen up his tongue."

"Did I loosen his tongue?" fenced the Lone Ranger.
He knew Vinton was pointing his words and acts toward a definite objective.

"You asked just enough questions, to find out all
there is to know about the express office and the murders. I wondered," he paused and looked at his glass
before continuing, "I wondered, if there was any particular reason for your curiosity." His eyes, like those
of a snake, fixed themselves steadily for a moment on
the face of the Lone Ranger. Though every muscle of
the mystery man was tense, ready for instant action,
his mask-like face seemed calm, relaxed.

"Is there any law against wanting to know what's
happened?"

Vinton shook his head slowly. "Nope. But there's laws against MAKIN' those things happen."

Baldy by this time, was straightening tables and chairs beyond the bar, oblivious to the conversation.

The Lone Ranger laughed carelessly. "You're barking up the wrong tree, Vinton! When a man drifts into town and has a couple of hours to kill, before the fun starts, what is there for him to do? I wanted to get inside someplace, and I couldn't hang around here without spending some money."

He thought Vinton's face became a slight bit crestfallen, but the change in expression was fleeting. Vinton at once took a new angle. "Plan to ride in the contests this afternoon?"

"I don't know."

"Those boots you're wearin', aren't much good for ridin'. D'you always wear such flat heels?"

"Not always."

"I once knew of a man that wanted to look a couple inches shorter than he really was. He wore flat heels."

"Is that so?"

"Um. And he blamed near broke his leg, when his foot slipped through the stirrups."

"Look here, Vinton!" There was a sharp note in the Lone Ranger's voice. "I've stood for just about enough of your suspicions. If you think I'm connected with the robbery in any way, say so."

"Nope. I reckon I won't say so, stranger, at least not just YET." With this, the sharp-eyed Vinton left the saloon, his drink untouched on the bar.

The Lone Ranger watched him as he pushed through the swinging doors. Through the dusty window, he could see Vinton step close to Silver. The suspecting Vinton ran his hand along the sleek flank of the horse, then scrubbed away the dry mud with a bandanna. He bent, and critically examined the snow-white hair, and when he walked away, he moved slowly, as if steeped in concentrated thought.

The Lone Ranger knew that Vinton suspected him of being the masked man who had fled the night of the robbery. He wondered if Vinton might not be some sort of special deputy left in town by Sheriff Potter to watch for suspicious-looking strangers. Vinton was certainly no fool. The explanation given by the Lone Ranger hadn't deceived him for a moment. The short conversation had been nothing but an introductory one. As long as he remained in town, the Lone Ranger knew, Vinton would probably make no further move, but, if he left, he would certainly be followed, or held by force. He didn't know that shortly after leaving the saloon, Vinton held a whispered conversation with another stranger in Black River.

Captain Skinner was a crook. The fact was obvious

to everyone. True, Skinner wasn't a highwayman, a bandit or a killer, but he probably profited more than many who were all three. Skinner was a gambler. As he stood talking to Vinton, he towered a full six inches over the black, sleek hair of Vinton's head. His long frock coat swung open to reveal one of the gaudiest vests that had ever been seen in Black River.

The thumb and one finger of his left hand hooked a lower pocket of the vest, while his right hand had a way of caressing the luxurious black mustache that drooped from his upper lip.

"So you suspect," he asked of Vinton, "that this stranger might be the one that left in such a hurry?"

"I'm sure of it, Skinner."

"Captain Skinner, if you don't mind, my friend." No one had ever heard where Skinner acquired the title, but he seemed quite proud of it.

"All right then, Captain Skinner. Anyway, I'm dead certain that's the man. There couldn't be two voices like that."

"Um, now that, my boy, is quite a remarkable bit of observation. I too, on the night of the robbery, noticed the peculiarly resonant depth of the masked man's voice."

"Well, the man in Baldy's has that same voice."

"Of course you must have been quite crude in your manner of questioning. You, my friend, are sadly lacking in the subtleties of the art of cross-examination." The captain stroked the mustache as he rolled his speeches out with polished grace, and an ease that was as glib as that of any confidence man.

"Oh never mind puttin' on the act for me," snapped Vinton testily. "You know that I'm not goin' to be taken in by it."

The tall gambler smiled down at Vinton. "I," he said, "will take matters into my own capable hands. I will learn the truth."

"How?"

"First, break down his guard and his defenses, by establishing a friendship. Then, in an unguarded moment, he may reveal the truth."

"Well, let me know as soon as he does."

"Perhaps you have visions of a reward, eh?"

"You know darned well I have."

"And why not?" agreed Captain Skinner.

The two left the place together, but outside they separated. The street was filling with people who were beginning to gather for the second of the several days that were grouped in the singular title "Frontier Day."

Skinner headed toward the saloon where Baldy worked, while Vinton moved in the opposite direction to meet his friend Brady who was to teach him the fundimentals of his job in the express office.

CHAPTER XIV

"A Challenge."

Once started, Baldy did more talking than the Lone Ranger cared to hear. He chattered constantly while the stranger in Black River tried to think out his plans. When he entered the town, he had no definite plan of campaign. He hoped to get the chance to examine the express office more thoroughly, but the suspicions of Vinton made this impossible.

Nothing Baldy had to say could shed more light on the identity of the thieves until he asked, "Is this Vinton crittur a friend of yours?"

The Lone Ranger shook his head. "No, I just met him here."

"Good thing. Yuh strike me as bein' a right sociable gent, but Vinton, now he's an ornery sort of buzzard. Mean as they come."

"Pretty shrewd though, isn't he?"

"Him?" Baldy guffawed. "He's jest so shrewd that he got took fer twenty dollars in as many minutes yestiddy by a crooked gambler that blowed intuh town."

103

He soused soiled glasses in a pan of water and wiped them to a high lustre before putting them on the pyramid of mates beneath the mirror. "No siree," he emphasized, "Vinton ain't the sense of a jackass."

Baldy certainly should know the men of the town, yet his statement contrasted strangely with what the Lone Ranger had thought when Vinton seemed to penetrate his disguise. He'd sized up Vinton, as a discerning individual. Then Captain Skinner swaggered into the saloon. He struck an attitude just inside the door and looked around. Then putting a solid gold toothpick between his lips, he strolled to the bar and ordered drinks. "And set them up for the stranger too," he said.

"Sorry," replied the Lone Ranger shortly, "but I don't drink."

Skinner looked at the empty glass and half-filled bottle that still stood before the Lone Ranger and lifted his eyebrows slightly. He said, "Suit yourself, Mister, but I always like to have company on my first drink of the day."

"This yere," blurted Baldy, "is a right fine gent, Cap'n Skinner." To the Lone Ranger he said, "Shake hands with my good friend, Captain Skinner. He's one of the best golblasted poker players that ever dealt a card in this saloon! I jest met him yesterday but we're good friends already."

Skinner acknowledged the effusive introduction with a slight smile, and met the hand of the Lone Ranger. "I didn't catch your name," he said softly.

"I didn't give my name."

"I see. Well, that's sometimes the custom, and no name at all, is every bit as good as something ... ah ... fictitious. You know, my friend, a lot of men around this part of the country left their names on the other side of the Mississippi."

His manner was pleasantly mild and disarming. Skinner was a likeable fellow, in spite of his questionable method of making a living. His heavy-browed eyes appraised the Lone Ranger. He must have decided that the nondescript clothes held little cash, and the clear, deep eyes of the Lone Ranger indicated anything but a man who might be easily fleeced. He apparently decided to postpone his business of the day until a more likely prospect appeared.

"If you haven't eaten your lunch," he invited with easy grace, "I'd appreciate your company."

Willing to grasp at any straw that might give him some information, the Lone Ranger accepted the invitation. Even though Skinner might not offer anything concerning the robbery, there was a chance that he might know a few facts concerning Vinton, and Vinton still bothered the Lone Ranger.

The two moved to a table and sat down.

The sun had broken through the drab sky, and the weather was rapidly improving. It promised fair for the games which began at two o'clock. This was to be the second day of the preliminary contests, held to eliminate some of the contestants. On the third and last day of the three-day celebration, the winners of the two previous days would meet in the final contests to determine the recipients of the various substantial cash awards.

Naturally, the talk between Captain Skinner and the Lone Ranger dealt to a large extent with the rodeo. "You know, my friend," said Captain Skinner, "that horse of yours should be competing. I suppose that's why you came here, isn't it?"

"I didn't plan to compete."

"I'm afraid, it might be wise for you to do so."

"Why?"

"Well, I uh—I have heard unpleasant rumours. A fellow named Vinton, whom I met at cards yesterday, told me confidentially that he is waiting for the contest, to prove a point."

"Did he tell you what the point was?"

"He did." Skinner paused for emphasis, and then went on. "He told me he suspected you might be able to tell something about the robbery the other night. Of course, he has no proof, but—." He left the sentence suspended.

"What have his suspicions to do with my entering one of the contests?"

"Simply this, my good friend. If you enter the contests, it would give everyone the chance to see your horse in action. Now let us say you enter one of the contests, your horse is mediocre, and Vinton would be satisfied that it was NOT the white horse that showed such speed in getting away the night before last. It would also establish a purpose for your presence in Black River. On the other hand, if you did NOT compete, you can see how it might be misinterpreted." The Captain was certainly a glib speaker. An actor too. The tone he used was almost apologetic. He regretted that anyone could have such suspicions about the tall man in the battered hat, and hoped sincerely that they would be allayed.

"You understand," he continued, "how Vinton might think you were afraid to exhibit your horse."

The Lone Ranger wasn't easily fooled. He knew that there had been a scant seven minutes between the time that Vinton left the cafe, and the arrival of Captain Skinner. He felt sure that Vinton had gone to meet this confidence man and gambler, and sent him here to test the theory he'd formed.

The Lone Ranger wondered, though, what made Vinton first suspect him. His disguise had always been fool-proof. What was there now, that betrayed him?

He knew that despite the casual manner of Captain Skinner, the gambler waited eagerly for his reply.

"I did come to town, with half a mind to compete in the contests."

"Good! I'm glad of that!" But there was a false ring in Skinner's enthusiasm. "The bronc-busting, perhaps?"

"No. The shooting."

Skinner frowned. "That doesn't prove very much. You won't need your horse in target shooting."

"But that's all I'm interested in."

A pause, while Skinner pondered. "Of course," he finally murmured, "it DOES give you a reason for being here. But you'd better," he made his words pointed, "be good enough at that shooting contest, to show you MIGHT have come here for that, and NOTHING ELSE." Skinner paused in a way that left no doubt as to his meaning. He concentrated his attention on his food for several minutes while he let the man across the table get the full importance of his words.

The Lone Ranger realized that Skinner had taken the buttons off the foils. He knew that it was up to him to prove, by his marksmanship, that he came to Black River to compete, and for no other reason.

"You see," went on Skinner to enlarge his challenge, "if you didn't have that as a reason for being here, there are a LOT of people who might think you just drifted in to learn whether or not anyone had a good description of the masked man who robbed the express office."

The Lone Ranger nodded slowly while he ate. The table manners of the gambler were impeccable. He handled both knife and fork, with an easy assurance and with the proper form that comes of long years of training in a well-conducted home. His manner, in fact, matched his meticulous speech and neat attire, except for one thing.

It was a small detail, that would perhaps have gone unnoticed by everyone, except the Lone Ranger, or perhaps Tonto. A detail, that at first seemed unimportant, yet one which grew in importance as the mystery rider thought more deeply. It was, in fact, a detail that would have a vitally important bearing on the developments of the next few days.

Skinner sipped his coffee slowly, when he finished eating. His luxuriant mustache caused him a little embarrassment and he apologized as he wiped it on a handkerchief. He muttered something about the place not supplying mustache cups, and guessed the meal might have been better served in the restaurant across the street. His apologies and suggestions, however, were lost on the Lone Ranger. That tall rider for justice was lost in his own thoughts. He had to get away from town. He had to meet Tonto, that was certain. How could he leave? He knew that Vinton, and if Skinner were aligned with Vinton, Skinner too, would leave him unmolested for a while, as long as he made no effort to get out of sight, but the first move toward escape would bring arrest, perhaps worse. At the moment, they had nothing more than strong suspicions on which to hold him, but escape would confirm their suspicions. Yet, he must escape.

CHAPTER XV

"THE PISTOL CONTEST."

While most of the rodeo events were dangerous only to the contestants, the pistol shooting match was different. In this, the ones least likely to be hurt were the contestants themselves, so the committee in charge took every possible precaution. The affair was staged outside of town, where a hill made a background to receive the bullets that went past the targets. The observers, judges and contestants ranged themselves on the opposite side of the valley.

As a further precaution every gun was collected by the committee and put in the safe-keeping of half a dozen men who were pledged to abstain from liquor until after the shooting was finished. There were always bets, and the resulting arguments, as to which bullet came nearest to the dead center of the bull's eye. Previous years had given the Black River committee vast experience in handling this particular contest. Even the spectators were forced to hand in their guns.

The targets were crude, but served their purpose. They were nothing more than slabs of wood, with half a dozen concentric circles painted on them. The small black circle in the center, the bull's eye, of course counted the most. As the circles grew larger, they counted less. When the slabs became riddled to the extent that they were on longer of service, they were replaced by fresh ones.

Each contestant used his own guns, which were loaded by the judges and handed out as each man took his turn. Five shots were considered a "round," and the total score of all five shots represented that man's standing for the round. The rules allowed that after each man took his turn, the six highest would take a second turn. Of these, two would be permitted to return the following day, for the final contest. The rest were eliminated. The same procedure had been followed the day before.

On the first day of the preliminary contests, about half a hundred people gathered to watch, while the rest gave their attention to the more exciting bronc-busting, riding, roping and bull-dogging exhibitions. The second day, however, when the Lone Ranger was to appear, there were fully two hundred men as witnesses. The box in which the spectator's guns were kept was filled to the top, and a second box more than half filled. Old "Whisker's" Finley, who flaunted a blue ribbon as custodian of the firearms, felt his importance on that day. There was a lively hum of conversation as the first round of shooting took place. In some way, the word had gone round, that the stranger in the battered black hat had decided at the last minute to enter the contests. There was an air of mystery about him. No one said he HAD stolen the gold from the express office, but there were several who whispered that he MIGHT have been the man, and one and all watched him with the feeling that he'd BETTER make a pretty darn good showing in the contest.

When he handed in his empty weapons to the judges, they examined them with widened eyes. A more beatiful pair of six-guns, they had never seen. The ivory butts were silver-mounted, and the balance, sights, and decorative markings, showed them to be weapons of a sort rarely seen on an ordinary cowman. Yet they made no comments. They broke the guns, and asked the stranger which he chose to use. They were told it made no difference. The guns, unloaded as they were, were immaculately clean. The inside of the barrels gleamed like polished glass.

The tall owner of the guns stood quietly, when it came his turn to shoot.

"You didn't turn in no ca'tridges," stated Dan Barker, the official.

"No!"

"I see yer ca'tridge belt is empty."

The tall man nodded.

"Too flat broke tuh buy lead, eh?" Dan Barker shoved five bullets in one of the guns. "Wal, yer entry fee allows yuh ten ca'tridges, of the size called fer by yer shootin' iron." He closed the gun, and passed it butt first to the Lone Ranger. "There yuh be, five shots, no more, no less. You finish among the first six an' yuh get five more."

The Lone Ranger nodded and gripped his gun. He walked firmly to the firing line. He hadn't been asked and hadn't thought it wise to tell, that he had cartridges for both guns in his pocket. But they weren't ordinary leaden bullets. They were of solid silver, the kind used only by the Lone Ranger. He wondered, if the change from silver to lead would make any appreciable difference in his marksmanship.

Those who went before the Lone Ranger, had shot well. The cash prizes were worth winning, and the best shots from all over the country were competing. He took plenty of time on his first shot, lining the gun's sights carefully. He held his breath and squeezed the trigger. His gun barked, to the accompaniment of laughs from many of the spectators.

He felt the crowd's antagonism. Men jeered and laughed at the time he had taken to aim, and compared it to the seemingly careless, but astoundingly accurate shooting of the other men.

It was one of the rules, that each contestant had the right to be told where every bullet struck, so if necessary he could make allowance for windage, and slight errors in his sights, on his next shot.

None of the contestants, however, had exercised that right. One had stepped to the white line marked on the ground with tape, and fired five times without more than five seconds between shots. The Lone Ranger, after his first shot, lowered his gun. "Please tell me," he said to a near-by official, "where that shot hit?"

The bow-legged man looked surprised. "Y . . . yuh mean," he stammered, "that you want me tuh go all the way across the valley an' then come back here, before you fire ag'in?"

"That's just what I mean."

"Wal, I'll be doggoned," muttered the other. Murmuring other, and stronger things, beneath his breath, he waddled toward the target. Jeers, cat-calls and shouts greeted the Lone Ranger's request.

"Scairt tuh death!" shouted one man, while another hooted. "What's the difference? You ain't got a chance anyhow. They's already two perfect scores."

The Lone Ranger tried to ignore the clamor, but found it hard. This sort of shooting was new to him.

He was, by nature, a modest man. His every act in the name of Justice, was done to help the worthy, and not for thanks or reward. He had always hurried from the scenes of his accomplishments, without waiting for thanks. Now, standing before almost two hundred pairs of hostile eyes, and as many antagonistic voices, he felt his confidence somewhat shaken. It was far, far different to fire at a distant target with nothing to be won but a cash prize, than it was to snap bullets from the hip and blast the gun from a killer's hands.

The bullets, too, were different. When he fired his own hard, perfectly-precisioned bullets of silver, he KNEW they would go where he aimed. Now, firing bullets of lead, and crudely cast ones at that, there wasn't the familiar confidence in his grip on the gun.

The official was returning, with a wide smile on his face. When still half-way across the valley, he held up his right hand with the thumb clamped down against the palm.

"A FOUR!" shouted a dozen men at once.

A bull's eye counted ten. The next ring was four, then three and two and one. The Lone Ranger's first shot had missed the bull's eye. The best score he could possibly get now, granting that all the remaining shots were perfect, was a forty-four.

"Which way did I miss the bull?" he asked.

"Half inch an' four o'clock!"

The Lone Ranger nodded. The shot had struck the target in the same relative place, to the bull's eye, that the number four would be on the face of a clock, and the shot was half an inch outside the highest counting circle.

Had Tonto been there to witness the shooting, he would have frowned and shaken his head slowly from side to side, unable to comprehend the fact that the Lone Ranger had missed the bull's eye.

Perhaps the light wind, blowing up the valley from the west, had been enough to deflect the shot. The Lone Ranger, when he generally fired, aimed more by instinct than by use of gun sights. Now, he was using the sights, trying to gauge windage, and trying desperately to win this contest.

He aimed his next shot a trifle to the left of the bull's eye, and slightly higher. In the terms of marksmanship, he aimed one half inch from the bull, at ten o'clock. His gun barked, and jumped, and once more the tall, grim-faced man requested a report on his shot.

The shouts that had greeted his last request, were like a gentle summer zephyr, compared to the tornado of jeers and cat-calls that came this time. The official's face grew red as he shouted above the clamour, "What're you tryin' tuh do? Make me walk my legs off?"

The Lone Ranger shook his head and repeated his

request in the same calm voice. The official's anger wasn't appeased a bit, when the shouting crowd began to clap hands in rhythm with each step he took.

Shading his eyes with one hand, the Lone Ranger saw the official step up to the target and examine it closely. Then the man turned, thrust both hands deep in the pockets of his trousers, and returned, while the delighted, laughing throng again clapped hands in tempo as he walked. This was what the delighted crowd had waited for. Something at which to shout, something to break the monotony of the long-drawn-out contest.

Bets were offered and accepted. Odds in every case were against the tall, lean-faced man in the tattered clothes.

"Yuh hit it that time," snarled the official.

"A bull's eye?"

"Umph." An affirmative grunt was the only reply.

"Where in the bull's eye? In the center, or slightly off?"

"What's the difference?" snarled the man with the badge. "I said you got a bull's eye, but it ain't goin' tuh do you much good, less'n you git three more."

The three remaining shots were fired with the same care and precision, but not with any too much confidence. The Lone Ranger didn't ask the blustering official to make another trip across the valley until he finished his round. Then another man brought back the report. "Four bull's an' a four," he called. "Total, forty-four."

The Lone Ranger walked to the table where the custodian of weapons sat, and turned in his gun. He, with five other men, were in the next round. Two of the others had scored fifty. Perfect scores. The best the Lone Ranger had done, was to tie with three other men for third place. But the all-important fact remained; he was to shoot again. That was imperative, because upon it, hinged his plans.

As he sat alone during the intermission, he reviewed those plans. There was that peculiarity he'd observed when Captain Skinner ate. That was the lead. There was the obvious alliance between Vinton and the Captain, also the fact that Vinton seemed to know him as the one who'd ridden from the express office after the robbery.

His thoughts and plans were interrupted when Captain Skinner himself appeared and sat down beside him. "Take it easy, my friend," began the gambler. "Don't let the crowd get on your nerves."

Skinner's manner was patronizing. He toyed with a medallion on the heavy gold watch chain that crossed the gaudy vest. "You're in the next round now, and you might be lucky."

"Lucky?" repeated the Lone Ranger.

"Of course," said Skinner. "Bates and Caulkins just MIGHT miss the bull's eye once, though in all the years I've seen them compete, I haven't ever seen it happen."

The Lone Ranger looked alert. "What did you say?" he asked.

Captain Skinner frowned. He didn't like it when people paid so little attention to his profound observations. "I said," he returned in a somewhat curt voice, "that I have been witnessing these contests for several years, and I have never seen John Bates, and Henry Caulkins, miss the bull's eye."

"That," said the Lone Ranger," is what I thought you said." With this somewhat cryptic remark, he left the captain sitting on the bench and walked over to the stand where the judges worked on tally sheets.

One of them, a jovial, big-faced fellow with several chins and little grey hairs sticking out of his ears, grinned at the Lone Ranger. "Well," he began in the first sincerely friendly voice the Lone Ranger had heard since he came to Black River, "you sure as thunder made that old grouch sore!"

"Who?"

"The target inspector!" Judge Bellows chuckled in a way that threatened at any moment to break into a huge laugh that would shake his ponderous figure. "I sure like a man that knows his rights an' stands by 'em. My name's Bellows, Judge Bellows, an' I'd admire tuh shake your hand."

"Thank you, Judge Bellows." The Lone Ranger gripped the large hand of the Judge, and was surprised to find it hard and firm, and not in the least bit flabby, as it might well have been, to match the jurist's figure.

The Judge went on talking, apparently not aware that the man before him hadn't given his own name. "Yes siree, lad," he said, "I'd like to see you beat the pants off them two cock-sure weasels, that got perfect scores. You all start even in the next round, an' you got just as good a chance as they have. Go on, show 'em they's a man can lick 'em at their own game."

"That's what I came to speak to you about."

"Eh? Reckon I don't understand."

"In the next round, I'd like to use both my guns."

"Fer what? Don't see as they's any pertickler reason fer usin' two guns. You only fire five times."

"I know, but I would like both guns, and I'd like to furnish my own bullets."

Judge Bellows's expression changed to something of a frown. He looked perplexed, and tugged at the wisps of hair on his right ear. His mouth puckered slightly. There was a peculiar quality about the stranger before him, that he couldn't understand. He picked up a sheet of paper on which the contestants' names were written.

"What name did you register for the contest under?"

"John Doe."

Judge Bellows ran a thick forefinger down the list until he came to, "Doe, John. Two guns, no cartridges. Score in preliminary, forty-four," he read.

"John Doe!" he finally exploded. "By thunder, there's something that ain't natural. I know enough of law, to know that that's the name that's used when there isn't any OTHER name to go by!"

The tall Lone Ranger nodded.

"What's more, it says here that you didn't HAVE no cartridges."

"Nobody asked me if I had any. I simply turned over my gun belt, and guns."

"Then you have some?"

The Lone Ranger brought his hand from a pocket, and held out about a dozen gleaming cartridges. Judge Bellows looked at them, then at the clean-cut face and steady eyes.

"Take one, and examine it more closely if you care to, Judge," invited the Lone Ranger.

The Judge accepted the invitation. He turned the silver bullet over in his fingers, then brought it closer for a more minute inspection. The rest of the officials at the table were interested in a keg of beer. They paid no attention to the conversation between the Judge and the Lone Ranger.

Bellows dug at the metal bullet in the cartridge with the nail of his thumb. He dug harder, but the silver showed no sign of any indentation, such as lead would have done.

During the inspection of the cartridge, which took several minutes, the Lone Ranger waited quietly. He saw Judge Bellows's face undergo a strange change, as he finally looked up.

"It sure is remarkable," muttered the big official, "how a man can hide his real face under a disguise. I lived in El Paso once, before I came here, and while I was there, I heard of a man that used Silver bullets. He rode a white horse. He called that horse "Silver" too."

"My horse is in that clump of trees behind you, with the other horses."

"Um-hum, thought it might be."

"I've been in El Paso," went on the Lone Ranger, his voice soft, and his words filled with meaning.

Judge Bellows looked grim. His face had lost the genial expression, with the understanding that this man before him was here, not to shoot a pistol for prizes, but for some more serious purpose.

"There's just one thing," he said. "This man I heard of in El Paso, was said to ALWAYS hit the mark."

"But not with unfamiliar weapons."

Judge Bellows nodded slowly. "The cartridges being a part of the weapons," he muttered. He held out his hand, with the cartridges he had been examining, looking very much alone in the broad palm. "You give me the rest of those bullets. I'll see that you get two guns, and I'LL LOAD THEM FOR YOU! Understand?"

The Lone Ranger understood, and dropped eleven more shots in the Judge's hand. It was significant that Judge Bellows took all TWELVE cartridges, and not just the five that were required for competition.

"You'll get what you asked for," he told the tall man softly. "I'll sneak it over on the other officials. But remember this . . . " and there was a threat in his voice, "if you're the man I think you are, you WON'T MISS THE MARK. Furthermore, I'll have a gun right here, trained on you. If you are NOT the man I think you are, but instead, happen to be . . . what Vinton and Captain Skinner HINT you might be . . . "

It was one more challenge for the Lone Ranger. It became more essential than ever, for him to shoot straighter than he'd ever shot before. He nodded wordlessly, and rejoined Captain Skinner for the rest of the intermission.

CHAPTER XVI

"FIVE SHOTS."

The six competitors drew numbers from a hat to determine their order of shooting. Judge Bellows himself held the hat, and passed it to each of the six in turn, the Lone Ranger last of all. No one noticed the deft bit of manipulation on the part of the Judge. He passed the hat to each of the men, holding it high, so they had to reach up and couldn't see the folded pieces of paper. While five of the men drew, there were but five slips in the hat. The sixth, the Judge let slip from between his second and third fingers, as the Lone Ranger drew. He drew a number six, and also drew a sly wink, from Judge Bellows.

It was a subtle deception, which hurt no one, and made it possible for the Lone Ranger to be the last to shoot. Judge Bellows couldn't explain to himself why he did it. He simply felt that whatever plan the man who had registered as "John Doe" had in mind, it would be to his benefit to be the last to fire.

New targets had been nailed in place during the intermission.

The official scorers took their posts, and the shooting contest got under way. The first man received his gun from the judge's table, and went to the firing line. He shot too quickly and scored only forty; four less than his previous attempt.

The second put his first four bullets in the center ring, but jerked the trigger on his last shot, and got a three . . . forty-three. The third, who had made the final round of shooting unexpectedly, had celebrated too soon with several swigs of liquor from the flask of a friend. His shots were scattered all over the landscape, and he retired in confusion, able to laugh at his futility with the good sportsmanship of the west.

"Reckon I'd o' done better," he commented with a wide grin, "if I'd o' used a shotgun."

Number four. A ripple of applause and shouts of encouragement greeted John Bates. "Git yerself five more bull's!" yelled one staunch supporter who had bet on him. Bates almost swaggered with conceit, as he strutted from the judge's stand, to the firing position. "That won't be hard," he replied to his backer. "All that's got to be done," he murmured, "is to allow for a little wind." He moistened his finger, and held it over his head while he calculated the breeze. It was simply a fancy gesture, as far as Bates was concerned. He'd heard of windage in the long-range rifle matches, but he'd never applied it to his pistol work. He was simply putting on an act for the benefit of the crowd.

Then he fired. His shots came in rapid succession, and it was almost perfect shooting. The five bullets struck the target close together, but something had happened to Bates. His exhibition had so impressed him, that almost subconsciously he HAD allowed for windage, and misjudged it. The five shots were off center, and only two of them struck the bull's eye.

"THIRTY-TWO!" shouted the scorer.

A moan from those who'd bet on Bates, and a loud yell of dismay from the deflated marksman. He tried to protest, shouting things about a double-cross, about someone tampering with his gun, and many other things, but the decision stood. Number Five.

Caulkins fired with care, and once more made a perfect score amid shouts and cheers. The Lone Ranger, the last to fire, would have to score five bull's eyes to tie Henry Caulkins, and to beat him, would have to group his shots not only in the bull's eye, but in the smallest circle, in the exact center of the bull's eye. At the distance, that was almost an impossibility.

The crowd shouted all manner of comments when he took his place. They saw Judge Bellows hand him two guns, and had much to say about it. Several of those at the Judge's table spoke, but Bellows, the accepted leader, silenced their protestations with the mere wave of a hand.

"What's the matter, cowboy, ain't one gun enough?"

"Mebbe he's afeared he'll be lopsided with only one shootin' iron, an' wants tuh keep on even keel." Laughter from the crowd.

"If yuh win the prize you better git a new hat."

"Yuh can't beat Henry Caulkins, whyn't yuh quit right now?"

These and other shouts rang from the crowd, while surly comments at close quarters came from the Inspector, "Make me look at the target after every shot this time, Mister, an' you'll be sorry for it."

Hard as he tried, it was impossible to disregard the clamour. The Lone Ranger, both guns holstered, took his place. His original plan, the one for which he'd entered the contest, had been to make a break, to shout to Silver, meet the powerful horse and race away from there, while every man was unarmed.

The rules of the contest which made the collection of the weapons essential, would have given him the chance to flee before Vinton, Captain Skinner, and probably many others who suspected him of being the killer and thief, could send hot lead to cut him down. Originally, he had no intention of actually shooting, in this second round. The prize meant nothing to him, even if he won it in the final round the next day.

But Judge Bellows made him change his plans. He

glanced toward the table, and saw the afternoon sun glint from blue steel in Judge Bellows's hand. The Judge held the gun lightly, almost carelessly, as if merely toying with an unloaded weapon, but the Lone Ranger knew the truth. He knew that gun in the Judge's hand was loaded, and that the Judge was waiting to be SHOWN, by the perfect marksmanship that was a part of his reputation, that he WAS the Lone Ranger.

Both guns still remained in leather, but now he drew one. His firm hand gripped the ivory handle. The bullets, he knew, were his own. The gun would fire with precision. But it was unfamiliar shooting. He had to make a perfect score, but it was his OWN security that depended on it. The Lone Ranger fought best, when he fought for others, for Justice or for the downtrodden. Now, if he failed, only he would suffer. His hand trembled slightly. The hoots of the crowd made fun of the time he took, as he stood there, waiting, hoping his hand would become steady.

He shook his head the least bit, then re-holstered his gun. He glanced toward Judge Bellows, and saw that big man's face looking hard, grim. The Judge didn't hold his weapon casually now. He gripped it, and held it steady on the Lone Ranger. A gun was levelled at him. He always shot best, when he fired into the very teeth of blazing gunfire. He recalled old

Ben Jenkins, and his cruelly tortured body. That was why he had to get away from here. He had to find the ones who murdered Ben. He had to prove some ideas that had come into his mind. He had to rejoin Tonto, regain his own familiar clothes, mask his face.

He had to ride on Silver, ride to Tonto's camp, then ride, and ride again!

Everything, the solution of the murder, the robberies, punishment of the killers, depended upon his getting away from town alive, and THAT depended on the next five shots he fired. If Judge Bellows didn't shoot him, no one else would be able to.

The shouts of the crowd faded into nothing. His ears closed to them. The surly chatter of the Inspector of targets became only a slightly monotonous drone, like that of an unnoticed fly. Once more he looked across the valley, at the target. The bull's eye looked bigger than before. The small circle in the center was clear and sharp. He straightened, the tension of his mouth relaxed. His hand came up with lightning speed. The gun came with it. He fired five shots from the hip. He didn't aim, he shot by instinct. He didn't need to ask where those shots went, he knew!

All five were fired in the space of two seconds. Shooting? Marksmanship? This was like neither one. This was accuracy, seen only when the gods of thunder send their lightning bolts to crash to the earth.

All five bullets tore through the target in the inner circle of the bull's eye, and a small coin could cover all the holes.

But that was only the beginning of the fast-moving chain of events that held the astonished on-lookers spellbound. As the fifth shot left his gun, the Lone Ranger snapped his other gun to bear on the crowd, and shouted in a ranging voice, "HERE SILVER!"

A whinny responded from behind the judge's stand, accompanied by a fast tatoo of hoofs, as a mud-caked horse burst from the trees, and raced to meet the marksman. As the horse came past, the Lone Ranger touched the saddle's pommel, leaped astride, and yelled once more, "Hi-Yo Silver, Away!"

Great racing strides—a flash of muddied white, and both horse and rider disappeared across the valley into the hills beyond.

It was the Judge who broke the stunned silence. He didn't speak, he yelled at the very top of his strong voice, "I KNEW IT! I knew it!" he whooped, with all his big chins shaking. Then, remembering, he finished his sentence to himself, "The Lone Ranger!"

CHAPTER XVII

"Back to the Mask."

It was a starry night, but very dark, with a soft wind whispering across the sage-brush, and sighing through the pine woods, where Tonto sat cross-legged in the shelter of the lean-to. He fed fresh sticks to the small fire. He had no intention of turning in to sleep.

The Indian could rest quite comfortably, and yet remain awake, alert and watchful. His every sense was tuned to catch the slightest sound that wasn't made by nature. Since the departure, that morning, of the Lone Ranger, Tonto had tried hard to be stoical. If anyone had been there to see him, they would have thought him quite calm. Yet, inside of him, there was turmoil.

Indians are frequently misunderstood . . . their control over their emotions is deceptive. Their impassive faces are seldom an index to their minds. Tonto was outwardly calm, but his feelings were a mixture of worry for the safety of his friend; of uncertainty as to the wisdom of going back to Black River.

The town by this time must be a seething torrent of revenge-thirsty citizens, demanding the life-blood of the men who killed and robbed. Sheriff Potter was no fool, and he would have returned to town. Jack Bannerman was exceptionally keen. The Lone Ranger had said so. And there were others, who might be even more of a peril to the Lone Ranger. Unknown others, the ones who had been inside the express office, while the masked man worked on the locked door. These men had had the chance to hear the voice of the Lone Ranger. Disguised though he was, the Lone Ranger's voice was distinctive, and might easily prove to be his undoing.

Yes, Tonto was indeed worried. After the Lone Ranger had left that morning, Tonto had packed the duffle and moved the camp to another woods, very close to town; a place that Sheriff Potter's men had already searched thoroughly. After Tonto had thrown up another small shelter, similar to the one of the previous night, he had mounted Scout and ridden to the trail. There, he placed three stones, one on top of the other, diminishing in size. A casual rider would pass without noticing them, but the Lone Ranger would be watching. He would leave the trail at the stones, and follow other blazes until he reached the new camp.

These activities occupied his time until noon. Then

he spent an hour, cleaning the mud and dirt from the clothes the Lone Ranger had left behind. Since then, Tonto's apprehension had increased. With the coming of night, he was torn between waiting there, as the Lone Ranger had instructed, or returning to the former camp-site. In the darkness, the Lone Ranger wouldn't be able to see the three piled stones. He'd have no idea where to look for this camp. But Tonto, in the end, decided to wait. It was the Lone Ranger who had given that command. "Wait for me," the masked man had told him. Tonto would wait.

He rose from the ground for the second time, and moved to one side of the lean-to. He brought out the familiar clothes of the Lone Ranger. The shirt, the dark trousers, the white sombrero, and the highly polished boots. The last trace of muck from the Devil's Bog had been removed hours ago. Tonto examined them once more, by the fire-light, to make sure no trace of the dirt remained. He knew none did, but the inspection gave him an excuse to handle the attire again. Tonto would have denied that he possessed the slightest trace of sentiment. Yet the manner in which he handled the Lone Ranger's clothing, was almost a caress.

He didn't replace them in the tarpaulin in which they had been wrapped. He laid them on the soft pine boughs that made a carpet in the lean-to. Then he once again left the vicinity of the fire. This time he went to his tethered horse.

Scout appeared to show the nervousness that Tonto felt, but kept suppressed. The pinto, though of course unable to reason, or understand what had taken place, sensed that all was not as it should be. Silver, the mighty stallion of the Lone Ranger, wasn't in the customary place beside him. Tonto could feel the horse's muscles quiver, when he placed his hand on a shoulder. At the Indian's touch, Scout reached around and muzzled the brown hand gently.

"Him come back, plenty soon," Tonto murmured, "or we go look-um for him."

Scout suddenly went rigid. His head came up abruptly. His ears cocked forward in attention. Tonto, catching the signal from the horse, dropped to the ground and placed one ear flat against the turf. There was a slight vibration. A distant tremor that might be made by a distant, hard-ridden horse. Rising, Tonto hurried to the shelter, took his carbine, and returned to the paint horse's side. Save for quivering muscles, and eager, trembling nostrils, Scout stood like a statue, motionless.

The hoofbeats were audible now, and coming closer. Sound carried a long way in the silence of the night. Tonto listened to the rhythm. The rider was traveling fast, he knew. Very fast. He timed the hoofbeats for a space of several seconds, and then his tension relaxed. He slapped Scout on the rump. "It all right," he told his horse. "No horse but Silver run that fast."

Tonto scooped an armful of light wood, and heaped it on the fire. The flames leaped high, to serve as a beacon for the approaching man. Tonto had no fear of bringing Sheriff Potter and his men. He knew from hoofprints that this camp had been one of the first place they had searched, and they had searched it with painstaking care. His great concern now, was that the Lone Ranger might ride by the camp. But such was not the case.

When the Lone Ranger rode in, he rode hard. "That fire!" he shouted to the Indian, "they'll see it!" He hit the ground and raced toward the lean-to. The fire made the inside bright. The mystery rider snatched off the battered old hat, the short, flat-heeled boots. He worked with frantic haste, pulling the false hair from his face, then washing the stain from his hair and skin. Tonto didn't need to be told to saddle Scout. He knew from the Lone Ranger's manner that they were to ride away from there together. Tonto didn't ask a question. What was to be told him, would be told in due time. The Lone Ranger began the explanation, as soon as his face was dry.

"I am suspected in town. I left there in a hurry, late this afternoon. There were men chasing me, but

I had a good start on them. I saw your sign on the trail, but didn't dare turn then. They would have seen the tracks. I kept moving, heading toward the Bog, then circled north and came back down this way after dark."

He had already changed his trousers, and paused in the explanation while he drew the fawn-colored shirt over his head. Tonto drew the cinch taut on his horse.

"The Sheriff and his posse are still out hunting us, but other men are a lot more likely to find us, if we don't get away from here before that fire brings them." He drew on his boots, then stood erect. "We haven't time to put the fire out, let them come. If we can have just one more minute, we'll be gone when they get here."

"Scout ready now."

"The duffle?"

"Got-um all hid."

"Then leave it hidden. We'll come back and get it another time. Tonight, we're traveling light, and fast."

The mask was now in place, and last of all the white sombrero. Then, buckling on his gun belts, which were filled now with the silver bullets, the Lone Ranger was once more the masked mystery rider. "Ready, Tonto?" he asked.

"Tonto ready. Me go-um with you?"

"Yes." The masked man gave the fire a quick inspection, made sure it wouldn't spread, then hit the saddle.

"We're going back," he cried, "back to Black River! Hi-Yo Silver, Away!"

CHAPTER XVIII

"THE SILVER BULLET."

Had Judge Bellows been anyone else, he would have found himself in jail. As it was, he spent a most uncomfortable afternoon and evening. Other members of the committee in charge told all who asked, that it was the Judge who had given the pistol contest winner two guns, instead of one. In the minds of the townspeople was no doubt, after seeing the flashing speed of the horse that carried the stranger away, and hearing the ringing shout of "Hi-Yo Silver!" that the one who had robbed the express office, and the matchless marksman were one and the same.

Vinton and Brady, the closest friends of the murdered Dick Tuttle, did their level best to arouse the people to the point of lynching the Judge. After all, hadn't he helped the stranger escape? Didn't this make him an accomplice? Failing in working the excitement to a lynching peak, Vinton and his friend demanded in the name of Justice, that the Judge be jailed and held till Sheriff Potter and Jack Bannerman returned.

139

But Judge Bellows was, after all, an important figure in Black River. He was one of the original settlers in the town, a man of wealth and background. For years, Judge Bellows had presided at the trials, and his wisdom in doling out punishment to fit the crime, was one of the boasts of the Black River people. They were angry at what he had done, but they felt that he was entitled to the chance to explain.

Imagine then, their consternation, when Judge Bellows said he had no explanation to make!

He left the scene of the pistol contest with a hundred men asking questions at his back. His home offered him no sanctuary. A score of people followed him into the big house, and hammered questions till long after dark. Meanwhile, men hunted for the man who had ridden away.

Judge Bellows wanted to explain. He wanted to tell the news at the top of his voice, but he knew the Lone Ranger wouldn't want it that way. He had no doubt that the Lone Ranger had actually been the one who rode from the looted office two nights before, but he was morally certain that it was NOT the Lone Ranger who had stolen the gold. One important point convinced him of this fact. One hundred thousand dollars worth of gold bullion is quite a load. Far more than two men can carry on a dead run, while they leap to the saddle of a horse.

The Judge was a bachelor. Ever since he'd settled in El Paso, long before he had come to Black River, the same couple had done his housework for him. An aged Indian woman did his cooking and cleaning, and her husband, the chores. Both lived in another building, furnished them by the Judge. The old squaw came into the huge living room around ten o'clock that night, to scold the men who still remained for not giving her master a chance to eat his dinner. At a gesture from the Judge, she took away the food and prepared to leave for the night.

Most of the men decided that it was a hopeless task to get an explanation, or any information, from Judge Bellows. Yet they all felt that he should be closely watched until the Sheriff returned.

It was Vinton himself who offered a suggestion, "We'll guard him all right," he told the men, "but there's no need for all of us to stay here. If four men stick with him, the rest of us can go an' do what we please."

The others heartily agreed with the suggestion. This was, after all, the last night in which to celebrate Frontier Day. Even though there was so much else to occupy them, the men didn't want to miss the activity in the saloons. And, too, a lot of them had bets to collect or to pay off. They didn't want to lose the cash in the former case, or be thought "welshers" in the latter.

"Do whatever you doggone please," Judge Bellows told the men. He lighted a fresh cigar, his tenth, and slumped a little lower in his comfortable chair before the fireplace. "If you want to stay here with me, make yourselves right at home. You'll find a bite to eat in the kitchen, more wood for the fire in the shed, cigars there on the table, and some first-class wine in the cellar."

"You needn't rub it in, Judge," muttered one of the men. "We don't have nothin' against you personally, but it's only that you oughta give some sort of explanation fer what you done in lettin' that killer git away."

"You'll get your explanation, when I'm ready to give it to you. Not before."

"Aw, shucks!" the lean-jawed man looked down. He gave his thumb-nail a critical inspection, shifted his weight from one foot to the other, and looked generally sheepish. "If you'd only be sore about the way we been questionin' yuh, an' the suspicions we been handin' out, you'd make us feel a heap better about guardin' you."

"Why should I be angry? I'd feel the same way myself."

A surly-faced man broke in, in a voice to match his face. "He's heapin' coals o' fire on our heads," he growled, "that's what the wise old coot is doin'. Wal, he ain't foolin' me none, or gettin' me off guard."

Bellows looked at the speaker with the first trace of a smile since early that afternoon.

"You be as nice as you durn please," the mean-voiced one went on. "Offer us victuals, wine, an' firewood, an' we'll TAKE it! If you git out'n that easy chair, I'll take THAT! We'll take all you want to offer, an' much obliged, BUT WE AIN'T LETTIN' DOWN OUR VIGILANCE!" He threw the butt of his cigarette into the fire savagely and turned to the other men. "Ain't that so?" he demanded.

The responsive nods told the Judges that no matter what happened, he was going to have house guests until the Sheriff returned.

The tall clock in the darkest corner of the room ticked off another hour. The conversation of the four guards dwindled off to an occasional muttered comment, and a monosyllabic reply. Just as if the four weren't there, Judge Bellows continued reading from a heavy calfskin-bound book on Trial Procedure. At eleven o'clock, he rose to toss another log on the fire, and while he was up, moved the single lamp a little closer to his book. Then he resettled himself and began another chapter.

"Tryin' tuh wait us out," grumped the surly-voiced man. No one bothered to reply. The large hand of the clock came close to half-past eleven, when it happened.

The five men leaped up when the window shattered just behind the Judge. Four of them snatched at heavy guns. The Judge's book fell to the floor with a thud, as he whirled quickly, despite his size. Outside, there sounded a clatter of hoofs, and a familiar shout, "Hi-Yo Silver!"

The men cursed and raced for the door, pausing only long enough to trigger shots at the fast-receding figure they saw through the broken window. They all knew that voice. They'd heard it the night of the express robbery. They'd heard it in the afternoon, after the thrilling pistol match. The resonant voice haunted them. Now it rang out once more and hinted that both searching parties were groping hopelessly for the wanted man, while he was right in town.

Judge Bellows wasn't concerned about the safety of the Lone Ranger when he heard the barking six-guns of his guards. He knew that the big white stallion had already carried the masked man out of range, and probably out of sight. As he turned once more to his easy chair, his eye fell upon a small, folded bit of paper between the chair and the window. When he picked it up, he noted its weight. Something was wrapped inside. A glance toward the door told him that the guards were still outside, explaining the gun-fire to other men who had joined them.

The paper when unfolded, revealed a cartridge . . .

a silver cartridge. It was a mate of the cartridge he'd loaded the brace of six-guns with that afternoon. The silver bullet had been wrapped in the note, in lieu of any signature. The note itself was brief. It took Judge Bellows only a moment to read it, then put it out of sight in one of his capacious trousers' pockets before his guards returned, more angry than before.

"Seems tuh me," snarled one, "you're doggoned unconcerned about havin' a winder smashed."

Judge Bellows finished a yawn before he answered. "You boys are worrying about me, and I figure there's no need of all of us being concerned. As long as you're going to take such good care of me, I reckon I'll go tuh bed."

He turned a broad back on them, and walked from the room.

CHAPTER XIX

"Judge Bellows's Rendezvous."

Reaching his room, Judge Bellows closed the door quite hard, then immediately opened it again. The latch clicked twice, in closing and opening, but the two sounds could be mistaken for one if the guards were bothering to listen. Then, squatting to the floor, he placed the heavy lawbook against the inside of the door to keep it from swinging open. The Lone Ranger's silver bullet, he wedged in between the door and the frame. When he stood, the door was firmly held, but it was open about half an inch, or the width of a .44 calibre bullet. Later, when he was ready to slip out of that door, he could open it softly, without a clicking latch to betray him to the men in the living room. Meanwhile, the door seemed closed.

The Indian woman had left a small fire in the Judge's bedroom fireplace. He tossed the Lone Ranger's crumpled note toward the flames, and prepared to carry out the masked man's hurriedly written instructions. The big jurist appeared to enjoy his work immensely, and went about his preparations with his eyes agleam like those of a schoolboy, sneaking out of the house at dawn on the morning of July 4.

From his wardrobe, the Judge chose old, but very companionable clothes. The clothes he generally wore for hunting or fishing. "Tonight's both hunting and fishing," he told himself. "Hunting for a clue and fishing for a killer!" He chuckled inwardly at the thought. When he had changed, he took a battered, old felt hat from the clothespress shelf. There were a dozen fishhooks stuck between the hat and the band. These he removed and laid on the wash stand. He put a pair of old boots by the door. He'd carry those until he was out of the house, and out of earshot of the four guards.

It took but a few minutes to pull down the counterpane on the bed, and make a bundle of clothes and extra blankets. With the bedding pulled back over the heap, there was a vague similarity to a sleeping man. But Judge Bellows frowned. The dummy wasn't very deceptive. He blew out the lamp, but the flickering fire was still sufficient to tell whoever might look into the room, that it wasn't the Judge's form that made the mound beneath the quilts. He could fix that, however. In addition to a wash basin, the marble-topped stand held a pitcher of water. He poured this on the fire, careful not to let it splash or hiss. Then he once more surveyed the room and the bed. The only light came from the moon and stars. There was a square patch of light on the floor near the single window, but the bed was dark. Just enough light, to show a heap upon the bed. Not enough to identify that heap. Once more Judge Bellows chuckled softly.

He put his ear close to the crack in the door, and listened attentively. He could hear the murmurs of the four men in the other room. A clink of glasses told him they had availed themselves of his invitation, and were enjoying his old wine. "They'll pay for it!" he murmured. The wine and the warmth of the fire would lull the guards to sleepiness. Their senses wouldn't be particularly keen, and they might even doze. That suited Judge Bellows perfectly. He sat on the edge of the bed and waited. He figured that half an hour would be enough to make the guards forget him. He didn't know it, when the thirty minutes was elapsed, but he was right. The guards had no thought of Judge Bellows. They assumed that he was sound asleep in his bed. They didn't hear a sound, when he finally rose, picked up his boots, moved back the lawbook, and stepped from the bedroom into a dark hallway. One end of the hall opened into the living room, the other went through the dining room to the kitchen, through the kitchen to the woodshed.

The door to the woodshed clicked slightly when the Judge went out, but not loudly enough to rouse the guards. In the woodshed, Bellows paused just long enough to draw on his boots, and locate by sense of touch, a spade. Then he went outside. Shouldering his spade, Judge Bellows made his way to the main street. Though almost midnight, things were still quite lively. The celebrants would not be as active as on the two preceding nights, because their supply of both cash and energy was running low. Another hour or two at most, would see the saloons closed. But the Judge had other things to do. Between now and two hours hence, there was grim work to be done.

Vinton and Brady spent the evening in one of the saloons. They nursed their drinks, careful not to take enough to make them careless in their speech. Brady appeared to be quite worried, but Vinton reassured him. "What are you worryin' about? The masked man's the one that'll hang for it."

"I'd feel better," Brady said, "if he was already hanged an' the case closed. As long as he's free, there's a chance that we might not get away with the robbery."

Vinton scowled. His beady eyes glanced at the man who was supposed to teach him the routine of his new job in the express office. Then he lowered his voice to an almost threatening tone. "Get this straight,

Brady," he said. "If there's any chance that you might turn yellow and squeal, say so now. You've got the chance to skip out of town, and stay in the clear. Otherwise, we might decide that you are too much of a risk for us."

Brady took a long sip of his drink. Fired with the liquor, he snapped, "Who's turning yellow?"

"You said you were worried."

"Well, I am. Anyone with any sense would be worried after what we had to do to old Ben Jenkins. I'm beginning to wonder if a hundred thousand is enough to pay for it."

"Thirty thousand," corrected Vinton. Thirty for each of us, an' forty for the man who schemed the whole thing."

"I don't see why he should get more'n we do."

"Because that was the agreement. Now let that settle it. If you don't like the deal, go tell Skinner so, and maybe . . . " Vinton paused, narrowed his eyes, and finished with pointed words, "maybe there will be only two of us to split the cash."

Brady checked an angry retort, when the waiter appeared at the table. "You gents aim to hang around all night?"

Vinton looked around him. Save for a couple of men who slumped with their hands pillowed on their arms atop the table, the place was empty. He tried to grin pleasantly, "Sorry, didn't know it was so late."

"I aim to close up as soon as I toss those drunks out."

Vinton rose, with Brady at his side, and the two sauntered into the night. The street was dark. Most of the other saloons had closed some time before.

"Before we go home," Vinton told his ally in the robbery and murder, "I want to check up with the boys at Bellows's home."

"That's another thing," replied Brady, unable despite Vinton's threats and reassurances, to keep his worries to himself, "I don't think it was at all smart to involve the Judge in this."

"What else was there to do? He helped that stranger get away!"

"But why did you have to take charge? Why couldn't you have let someone else suggest a lynching, and when that didn't pan out, suggest jailing him? Why didn't you let the idea of keeping the Judge guarded, come from someone else?"

"Oh forget it. We've got to try and act natural, don't we? Isn't it natural, that with your friend Ben murdered, and Dick Tuttle, a friend of both of us, murdered, we'd naturally be the ones most anxious tuh see the killers pay for it? The Sheriff and Jack Bannerman are out huntin' for that masked man. There's no one else particularly interested in seein' justice done . . . other than us."

"I don't want to see JUSTICE done," Brady insisted, "I want to see that masked man hang, and the case closed up."

"He'll hang as soon as he's found. I only wish I'd closed in on him, when I recognized his voice, while he was here disguised."

The two were walking toward Judge Bellows's home.

"Why didn't you?" asked Brady.

"Because Skinner said not to. I'm taking orders from Skinner. If we'd captured him, he'd have been stowed away in jail. He'd have been held for trial . . . and then someone, maybe Judge Bellows himself, might have wondered WHERE WE WERE, THAT WE COULD RECOGNIZE HIS VOICE! We were not in that bunch that came up with the Sheriff. Maybe someone would have guessed that we were INSIDE that office."

"By thunder," exclaimed Brady, "that's a point I'd never have thought of."

"Course you wouldn't. That's the reason we're goin' to be in the clear, with Skinner makin' all the plans. He wanted to keep this stranger in sight, till we could find him with his mask and his other clothes, THEN we could have shot him. That would have ended the whole thing."

Halfway to the Judge's home, the two conspirators

met Captain Skinner, who told them about the exciting episode of several hours ago, when the masked man appeared at Bellows's house. "You'd better go there," he concluded, "and check up on the guards."

"I was aiming to anyhow," replied Vinton. "Why don't you come along, Skinner?"

The gambler shook his head. "Not me. Remember, my friends, I am a stranger in Black River. I have little interest in your local crimes . . . and criminals." He laughed softly. "Little interest! Only about a hundred thousand dollars worth."

"When," asked Brady, " do we get the money split up?"

"When I feel it will be safe," was the softly spoken reply.

The captain left them, while the pair went to Judge Bellows's home.

"We're takin' turns at guardin'," one of the four men told Vinton. "They ain't no use all four of us stayin' awake. Me an' Sam will stand watch till about three a.m., then we'll git us forty winks while Lem an' Snag stand watch."

Vinton looked angry. He was angry. The empty wine bottle, soiled glasses, the chicken bones that told of a tasty snack of cold meat and the pile of thick cigar butts told a story of a pleasant night. Sam blew a fragrant cloud of cigar smoke toward the ceiling and grinned toothlessly at Vinton.

"The Judge sure treated us white," he explained. "Told us to make ourselves right tuh home, an' went to bed."

"Is he in bed now?"

"Reckon so. I dunno where else he'd be."

"Do you mean to say you haven't even bothered to take a look at his room?" Vinton grasped eagerly at the chance to criticise the way in which the guards had conducted their vigil. Perhaps his selfish nature made him more jealous of the luxury they'd enjoyed than he cared to admit.

"Shucks, Vinton," it was Sam who spoke, "why wouldn't he be in bed?"

"He probably is, but you shouldn't have given him the chance to slip out. Come," he picked up the lighted lamp, "we'll go and have a look."

Vinton hadn't the slightest suspicion that Bellows would be anyplace else but in his bed. He felt his authority, and got an inner thrill in asserting it. After all the months, during which no one had given him any attention, it was fine to see men take his orders. Sam rose, and followed Vinton down the hall. Brady was close behind him. Pete Merwin, the other guard on duty, didn't bother to get out of his comfortable chair. He simply muttered something about a "Dog-

goned upstart," lighted a fresh cigar, and settled back
to enjoy its aroma. But a sudden shout snapped him
to his feet. The two who slept wakened with a start
and raced after Pete Merwin, toward the Judge's room.

Vinton's face was livid with rage, when he saw the
Judge's deception. The heap of quilts and clothing lay
exposed where he'd snatched back the counterpane.
In the midst of a snarling curse, he broke off sharply,
and pounced upon a bullet near the door. He didn't
know the significance of the silver bullet, but he
shoved it in his pocket to consider later on.

It was Sam, who found the message in the fireplace.
It was the note, sent by the Lone Ranger to Judge
Bellows. The Judge, in throwing water on the fire,
unthinkingly saved the most important part of that
note, from the flames. Vinton, reading it, let out a
whoop.

"WE GOT 'EM!" he shouted. "This is from the
masked man. First part of the note's burned up, but
the part that's here, says to meet at half-past two, behind the express office. They'll be meetin' there, inside
of the next few minutes. AND WE CAN SUR-
ROUND THEM. TRAP THEM!"

"How d'you know it's from the masked man?"

"Who else could send it? This proves the Judge is
in cahoots with him. We'll cut 'em down with hot
lead. Come on!"

The others followed Vinton, drawing their guns as they did so. Brady alone, knew the masked man was NOT guilty. What was he going to tell Judge Bellows at this rendezvous?

CHAPTER XX

"MASKED MAN'S PLANNING."

Tonto was as silent as a shadow when he moved through the darkness in town. The Lone Ranger had given the Indian the most specific of instructions, based on knowledge gathered in the day he'd spent in town. Tonto knew just where to go, to find Captain Skinner's boardinghouse. He knew that by creeping softly behind the row of buildings fronting the street, he could reach the solidly built, two-story house where Mrs. Prindle lived. He knew that when he reached this house, the first floor window in the southeast corner, would give access to the room that Captain Skinner rented.

Tonto crouched beneath the window, and began a long vigil. One hour passed, and then another. He tried to compute the time. It must have been around nine-thirty, when he and the Lone Ranger had hurriedly abandoned their last camp. Half an hour had taken them to Black River. Another half hour must have been consumed in reaching this post. Shortly after he took his place, he heard the distant shouts, and the cry of the Lone Ranger came faintly to his ears. Then the time began to drag. The Indian was irked at the inactivity of his part in this affair. So far, the Lone Ranger had carried the burden of activity, but if tonight's events went forward according to schedule, Tonto's chance for action would come soon. With this thought, the Indian consoled himself, and waited through the dragging hours. It was well past midnight, when a patch of light flashed from the window, and framed a square of ground. The bedroom's occupant had finally arrived. Tonto rose from his position and peered over the sill of the window. Captain Skinner stood beside the lamp he'd lighted, replacing the glass chimney.

Tonto watched the confidence man for several minutes, in accordance with the carefully detailed instructions of the Lone Ranger. Then, from beneath his blouse, he drew a length of rope. One end, was fashioned in a noose. His powerful fingers felt the noose, made sure it ran smoothly, then opened it wide. He laid the coiled lariat on the ground a few feet from the window, against the foundation of the house, where he could reach it quickly in the darkness. Then, knotting his fist, he tapped lightly several times on the house.

He heard the sound of motion come from Skinner's

room. He rapped again, and then the window opened. Tonto crouched in the shadowed angle made by the house and the ground, practically invisible. He watched intently, heard a soft mutter from Skinner, then he tapped the house again.

His fingers gripped the rope. A louder growl from Skinner, then the head and shoulders of the Captain appeared outside the window.

Tonto gave a quick flick of his wrists, and the lariat snaked out with lightning speed and unerring aim. Before Skinner was aware of it, the rope had settled around his shoulders and Tonto had jerked it taut.

"What the . . ." choken Skinner. The rest of what he had intended to say was broken off, as another jerk of the rope brought him sprawling from the room, to land with a hard thud on the ground. Dropping the rope, Tonto scrambled over the prostrate gambler, and clamped a hard, strong hand against the mustached mouth.

Skinner was no weakling. He struggled furiously, but he was no match for the iron sinews of Tonto. This was the first time in many days, that Tonto had had the chance to use his strength against an adversary, and he gloried in the incident. He turned the gambler flat upon his back, then held him down by planting a knee on each shoulder. Captain Skinner lay almost motionless. Then, as Tonto moved his hand from the man's mouth for just a moment, Skinner took a deep breath, but before he could shout, a gag was jammed between his teeth.

Then, with both hands free to work, it took Tonto only an instant, to coil the lariat around the other man, and pinion his arms to his sides. Skinner's own belt served to lash his ankles together.

Then Tonto stood, grinning widely, and surveyed his work. The light from the window fell on Skinner's face. His eyes showed stark terror. Tonto grabbed the tall man's heels, and dragged him roughly across the ground, where he'd be less in evidence if someone should chance to come by. Then he climbed in through the open window. Using more care with Skinner's clothes, than he had with Skinner himself, Tonto took them from hooks and hangers, and packed them in a pair of brand new handbags he dragged from beneath the bed. Then he looked around the room, to make certain none of the Captain's property had been overlooked. He opened the door of the room softly, and listened for a moment, to make certain none of the other occupants of the house had been disturbed. Satisfied, that his work was done with the quiet efficiency that the Lone Ranger had cautioned him to use, he closed the door and lowered the valises through the window to the ground outside. After blowing out the candle, he, too, left the room.

A glance convinced Tonto that Skinner was sure to remain where he was for the next few moments, then the Indian companion of the Lone Ranger picked up the bags, and walked toward the woods a couple hundred yards away. When he returned, a little while later, he came empty-handed. This time, he lifted Skinner bodily, and carried him across his shoulder like a sack of wheat. Skinner tried to struggle, but the hard grip of the Indian warned him that struggling would bring nothing more than pain, so he permitted himself to be lugged to the woods, tossed across the back of Tonto's paint horse, and carried, with Tonto in the saddle behind him, out of the town.

There was grim purpose in the way Vinton, Brady and the four men who had been left to guard Judge Bellows, stalked toward the express office with guns drawn. Vinton took charge of the small party. The others seemed ready and willing to follow his instructions.

"When we get to the office," he told them, "We'll split in two parties. Brady will take two of you, and you two," he pointed to a couple of the men, "will go with me. We'll sneak up on that meetin' from two sides an' have our guns ready. Shoot at the first attempt to make an escape."

Brady nodded. The others didn't feel that an answer was required. Each of them, however, secretly promised himself that if he had to shoot he'd certainly not shoot to kill Judge Bellows. They seemed certain that there must be some sort of explanation for the peculiar actions of the old Judge, and were willing to await his readiness to give that explanation.

"Quiet now," cautioned Vinton, as they came nearer their objective. "We'll slip up to the porch, then we'll split, and three of us go around each side of the office." He slipped his gun from the holster, and cocked the hammer. The faint click sounded menacing.

The Lone Ranger was engaged in hurried conversation with Judge Bellows. The big white stallion, Silver, stood close by the two men, there in the darkness. The Judge still held his spade, but now there was moist earth clinging to it. He did most of the talking, while the masked man listened, interrupting only when he asked a short, terse question. From time to time, the Lone Ranger nodded, and his face grew increasingly grim. "Most fiendish plot I ever heard of," he murmured once.

The Lone Ranger's hand, resting on the pommel of his saddle, felt Silver suddenly stiffen. It was a warning, but he was too keenly interested in what Judge Bellows said, to heed it. Rarely, did the Lone Ranger make a mistake of this sort. He couldn't afford to. His slip that night, behind the express office would have cost him his life, if Vinton hadn't been too eager to kill.

The first intimation the Lone Ranger had of danger, after Silver's silent warning, was the shot. The orange flame of Vinton's heavy gun, lashed from one side of the office. The bullet tugged at the masked man's shirt sleeve as it buzzed angrily by. Shouts came from two directions at once. Shouts demanding immediate surrender. But the Lone Ranger was in action. With the bark of Vinton's gun, he realized the situation. Before Judge Bellows could recover from the first shock of surprise, the Lone Ranger's fist arched in a short hook, to land flush on the heavy jurist's jaw. Judge Bellows didn't know what struck him. He dropped to the ground, unconscious. Then Vinton fired again, but this time, he shot at a moving target. The Lone Ranger vaulted to the saddle and Silver was away like a streak of white flame, flashing through the night.

Six men raced toward the fallen Judge. Vinton's angry shouts of "KILL" rose high and shrill above the others' voices. He sent two more shots winging after the masked rider, then tried to bring his gun to bear on Bellows. "NO YUH DON'T," cried one of the four who had been guards. "He's down on the ground and out cold. You cain't shoot a man in that sort o' condition."

"Let go my arm."

"Not on yer tintype, Vinton. We'll take the Judge intuh custody, lock him in jail if need be. Reckon we got reason enough tuh do that now, but I'm durned if I'll let you drill him."

Vinton struggled briefly, but he saw that all four of the guards were agreed on what the speaker had said. Brady offered no comment either way. "All right then," he finally snarled, "BUT LOCK HIM UP."

When Judge Bellows heard later just what had happened, he felt grateful. The quick-thinking that had brought the Lone Ranger's fist to strike him down, had unquestionably saved his life. The Lone Ranger, far better than any other man, knew and understood the code of the west. Judge Bellows was headed for jail, but at least he left the scene of the rendezvous alive.

None of the men, departing with their prisoner, had the slightest suspicion that the Lone Ranger would return that night. Yet that is precisely what the daring masked man did. He had one more detail to attend to, and if the capture of the Judge didn't ruin his carefully laid plans, that detail would be a vital one. He came as close to the express office as he dared, then dismounting, he left Silver tethered to a tree, and came the rest of the way on foot. Everything was quiet now. It took him several minutes to locate the Judge's spade. When he found it, he took the tool to the room where Captain Skinner had lived until he was carried away by Tonto. The window was still open. The Lone Ranger could easily reach over the sill. He struck a match, and one glance told him all he needed to know. Nothing belonging to Captain Skinner was in sight. Tonto had fulfilled his part in the night's activities. The masked man placed the recently used spade beneath the bed, then slipped out once more, into the night.

CHAPTER XXI

"THE GOLD IS OURS."

The contests on the last day of Black River's celebration, fell flat. True, they were hotly contested, and won by skilled men, but after the exciting events of the preceding day, when the mysterious stranger had ridden off, the winning marksman; the suspicions against Judge Bellows, and the culminating excitement after the town had gone to bed, the bronc-busting, bulldogging, roping and shooting finals seemed an anticlimax. The officials hurried the events along, as if they were a necessary bit of troublesome routine that had to be disposed of, before they could go and see Judge Bellows.

The Judge grinned comfortably in the jail. At his request, Vinton left the same quartet of guards on duty, and these men, when told that the Judge himself would feed them, eagerly accepted the assignment.

There were countless stories about the affair of the night before. Though he tried hard to play the role of hero, Vinton found that most of the townsmen some-how managed to blame him for the disgrace of Judge Bellows.

The solid older citizens pleaded with the Judge to tell all he knew about the masked man. They assured him that they were on his side, that they were certain he was entirely free of all wrong-doing, if only he would explain. To all who came to talk and cajole through the bars, the Judge simply waved a ponderous hand. "When the time comes, boys, I'll tell my yarn."

He felt safe in jail. Nothing would persuade the men to harm him, until he'd been hauled into court by Sheriff Potter, and that couldn't be done until the Sheriff returned. There was still no sign of the posse that included Jack Bannerman, when the sun went down.

Most of the visitors left soon after the contests were finished. Saloons and restaurants were silent again after the turmoil of the last few days. The men who had ridden after the Lone Ranger, when he fled from the pistol contest, returned and told about the finding of his discarded camp and discarded clothes, the old clothes, that he'd worn when they saw him last. They heard with dismay about his return during the night, and they too had a session through the bars with Judge Bellows. But like all the rest, they failed to gather the slightest shred of information from the Judge. The worry on Vinton's face, as he moved about the town, grew deeper.

At the dinner hour, he sought out his friend Brady, and the two compared notes while they ate. "What d'you think has happened to Skinner?" he asked.

Brady didn't know. "I haven't seen him since last night. The chances are he's sleepin' in all day today." Brady seemed less concerned than Vinton, but Brady didn't have Vinton's suspicious disposition. "Did you go to his boardin' house?"

Vinton shook his head. "It's just as well if we don't seem too well acquainted with him. Remember, he's a newcomer to town."

Brady nodded. He pushed back his plate with his meal almost untouched. He was losing interest in the whole affair. Probably, he would have welcomed the chance to be out of it entirely, even though it cost him his share in the loot.

But Vinton wanted the money. He wanted to keep close tabs on Captain Skinner until the final division of the spoils. Various remarks and suggestions of the confidence man, kept recurring to him, and he could catalog them all, now that he began to feel apprehensive, under the classification of suspicion. "Skinner," he said, "seemed to stall an awful long time about dividin' that gold."

"Umm," murmured Brady.

"It was his idea that we wait until the celebration was finished, before we made a move to take it away from here."

"That's so." Brady drummed with a fork on the edge of the table, and leaned back in his chair.

"I wonder if Skinner would have sold us out, and tied up with the masked man?"

"The whole idea was Skinner's from the start," offered Brady. "I didn't like it at all, as you remember, but he talked us into it."

"That's so. Now that we've done our part, he could have worked with that masked man, and split the stuff two ways, leavin' us out in the cold."

"And what could we do about it?"

"That's just it." Vinton's beady eyes grew sharper as his suspicions became better founded. "And they might have had the Judge to help them, too! He's sittin' in jail, lookin' mighty well pleased with himself. Probably he figures he'll get his cut later on."

By this time, Brady too was worried. "If that's the case," he said, "the sooner we find out about it, the better. I'm not goin' to hang around this town, and let them stick my neck in a noose!"

"Me neither." Vinton rose from the table decisively. "I'm callin' on Skinner whether he thinks it's safe or not. Come on."

"I'm with you."

The two flung out of the cafe, tossing a couple of coins on the bar. They headed directly for Mrs. Prindle's house. A sign on the door told them that there were rooms to rent. Three strides took them up the steps, and Vinton hammered at the door.

Ma Prindle herself came to the door, and it was obvious that she was angry. As soon as she saw Vinton, she put both big, work-reddened hands on her hips. Her beefy forearms were bare to the elbow. "Wal," she began, "it's a fine sort of crook you brought here to take a room from me."

Vinton felt even more alarmed. "Wh . . . what's the matter?" he faltered.

"Matter aplenty. I should have knowed better'n to take in a gamblin', schemin', slick-talkin' coyote like that without gettin' my money ahead of time."

"HE HASN'T LEFT!"

"The heck he ain't. He slunk out like a prowlin' coyote durin' the night. Went out the back winder, and took his bag an' baggage with him."

"Why the . . . " but Vinton checked himself. He didn't dare show too much concern. He had to guard every speech, lest some carelessly dropped word or action betray him. His brain was whirling at the verification of his suspicions. He barely heard Ma Prindle saying, "I'm goin' to make you pay fer his room."

"Y . . . yes, sure thing, Mrs. Prindle." It was Brady who in this emergency found his tongue first. "We'll see that you don't lose anything."

The big woman's round face softened slightly. "I don't like to be mean about it," she said, "but you gents know that I can't afford to lose a week's room rent, an' the son of a snake ate enough fer two men. Took his breakfast an' dinner here most of the week."

"Didn't he leave anything at all behind? Nothing?"

"HUMPH!" the landlady snorted, "Left nothin' of any value! An old spade, that's all."

"A SPADE!"

"Yere." She reached behind the door, and brought it out. "And he wasn't even decent enough to fetch that in clean. It was all packed with half-dried mud, an' the floor of his room was a sight. Mud all over the new rug I hooked last month."

The spade may have looked innocent enough to Ma Prindle, as she showed it to the two men, but to them, it represented the loss of a fortune in gold. One hundred thousand dollars, must have been dug up and carried away by the double-crossing Captain Skinner. Vinton said nothing, but Brady mumbled a few words about paying sometime for the Captain's room. The two left, almost staggering under the weight of the blow. Now that the gold was actually gone, Brady felt the loss too.

"Got to be sure, got to be!" mumbled Vinton, as the evil pair walked along the street. "Got to be sure he got it. Maybe he didn't!"

"Sure he's got it," growled Brady. "That's why he skipped out of town."

"But maybe he didn't take it all. He might have left our share."

"Slim chance of that!"

"But I've got to be sure. That's a heavy weight to carry on a horse. Maybe he's hidden it somewhere else. That must have been what the masked man and the Judge were talking about last night." Vinton talked rapidly, practically thinking out loud. His words were disjointed, disconnected, and sometimes mumbled. "Skinner, the masked man and the Judge! It all ties up. Bellows knows we're the only ones that know the truth. He knows we can't squeal. We killed a man, he didn't. We'll hang, he won't. Double-crosser . . ." He stopped in his tracks and jabbed Brady on the chest. "Listen," he spoke softly, "we're going to learn the truth. Tonight, we're going to dig and find out! You meet me at the cemetery, with a couple of spades."

"What time?"

"Tonight, at midnight."

Most people retired that night as soon as it was

dark. They were exhausted after the three-day session, and welcomed a good night's sleep. Had they dreamed of what was going to happen between midnight and dawn, no power on earth would have driven those townsmen to their homes. But who could foretell the actions of the Lone Ranger? Not even Tonto, and certainly the usually peaceful folk of Black River had not that power.

Vinton and Brady saw no signs of life, as they moved through the street. They rounded the express office at the end of the main road, and continued past it for about a hundred yards. They came to a low white fence, surrounding the graves of several hundred people. Silently they moved through a small gate, which they left open, and then into the sanctuary of the plot where a pale moon washed the crude markers with silvery light.

There were several graves of recent making. The grass hadn't yet grown over them. The first two, Vinton and Brady passed by, but they paused and squatted beside the third. Vinton let out a low, but fervent curse. "This ground's been dug up recently," he told his partner.

Brady felt a handful of the soft ground, and nodded. "Mebbe so, but we got to make sure, don't we?"

Vinton rose, and started digging. Brady on the other side worked with him at a feverish pace. The soft ground flew, with neither man caring where it landed. They had no intention of replacing it. Let the hole they dug, remain. Whatever was buried beneath the ground there, would soon be removed. They simply hoped that there would be SOMETHING buried.

After a long session of silent digging, Vinton's spade struck something hard.

"THE BOX IS HERE!" he exulted to Brady. They increased their pace, sweat streaming from their faces. The grave was one of the usual depth and size. It took some time, and vast energy, to lay the six-foot wooden coffin bare. Then it took more time, to get room to open the lid without hauling the big box from the pit.

Finally, Vinton paused a moment, and glanced tensely at Brady. Then he called, "Now, we'll see!" His lean face in the moonlight, was a ghastly sight, streaked as it was with sweat and dirt, and expressing an almost frenzied horror that his worst suspicions were to be realized.

"Can you open it now?"

"One . . . one second," grunted Vinton from the hole. His voice told of straining effort. There was a little squeak as the lid moved on the hinges. "I'm . . . getting . . . it!" Another tug. A moment's suspense, while Vinton struck a match, and looked inside the coffin.

"THE GOLD IS HERE!" He laughed, in a state of mind that bordered on hysteria. "It's here, it's all here! Every bar of it!"

"THE GOLD IS OURS!"

CHAPTER XXII

"Conclusion."

Vinton's hysteria was contagious, and his partner Brady caught it. The sight of gold does strange things to certain types of men. The two killers struck match after match to feast their eyes on the bars of glittering metal, in the otherwise empty coffin. They were so intent on their discovery, that they didn't hear the barely inaudible sound of men approaching. The first realization Vinton had that anyone but he and Brady were in the little cemetery, was the sharp command, "Lift yer hands, an' keep 'em high!"

It took a moment for full realization to come to Vinton. He was brought back from the clouds of rapture with a sudden jolt, and when he finally looked in the direction of that voice his jaw went slack, his beady eyes went wide, and his voice stammered, "T . . . the . . . the Sheriff!"

"Sheriff is right!" barked Potter. He took several steps toward the startled pair. Close behind him came Jack Bannerman, then a tall man whose face was partly covered with a mask, and an Indian. Other men stood behind the group.

Bannerman began to speak. "You dirty, schemin' skunks!" he bellowed. "Schemin' to rob me, plottin' the death of Ben Jenkins! Framin' another man fer your guilt, an' all the while posin' as friends. YOU," he roared at Brady, "makin' out to be so honest!" His big fist was knotted at his side. Brady tried to step back, but Bannerman's hand shot out, to grab a fistful of the clerk's shirt. "Killin's too good fer you!"

"Wait! Wait," pleaded Brady. "I didn't like the scheme from the start, but I had to go in on it!"

"Yer not only a crook, a coward, an' a killer, but a lyin' rat tuh boot!" Rage shook the big frame of the manager of the office. "I oughtta smash yer face in right here an' now."

"Take it easy, Bannerman." It was a calm deep voice that spoke. The Lone Ranger stepped forward, and gripped Jack Bannerman's arm. "He'll get all that's coming to him."

Bannerman relaxed a little, and let go of Brady's shirt. "I . . . I reckon yer right, stranger."

"I'll take the two of 'em in hand," declared the Sheriff. Vinton attempted to argue still, despite the damning situation in which he'd been caught. "That masked man's the one," he howled at the Sheriff. "He's the one that done it."

Potter simply laughed. "Yuh blamed fool. If he done it, what d'you suppose he trailed us all day tuh fetch us here for?"

"T . . . trailed . . . YOU?"

"That's what he done. Soon as we seen him, an' that Injun friend of his, we all snatched guns, but he told us where we was fools not to stop an' reason things out. No man alive, could have toted all the gold there was away with him that night. We seen him an' the redskin run from the office, an' just took it for granted he had the gold. Never stopped to think, he couldn't have lugged it."

Bannerman took up Potter's story. "Just in case you try an' hand out some more fancy lies, let me tell you JUST WHAT YOU DONE. You first killed old Ben, figgerin' to get the plans for shipment of the gold. Then you figgered out a better scheme, when you seen the plans wouldn't give much chance to steal the gold. You got it all out'n the safe, an' hid it somewhere outside. Then you fired some shots, figurin' to fetch men racin' from the saloons. That's just what happened. You cooked up a story about Dick Tuttle havin' been shot. That went over, because everyone was too drunk to look close at his body. The Doc, an' the Coroner was likkered too. You hurried through the buryin'. But you put the gold INTUH the coffin, after you let Dick Tuttle out."

Vinton gasped, as Bannerman drew a breath, and continued. "The only trouble was, that this masked man was outside the office, havin' learned somethin' from old Ben before he cashed in his chips. He was IN the office two seconds after you fired the shot and vamosed. HE DIDN'T SEE NO ONE DEAD. No sign of anyone bein' wounded. That's what set him thinkin'."

"Wait, Sheriff," Vinton broke in. "It was Dick Tuttle. He planned it all! He made us help him, then he got scared an' cleared out."

A harsh, humorless laugh came from Bannerman at this statement. "Catched in a lie at every turn," he shouted. "Yuh dirty whelp, Dick Tuttle is in the hands of the law right now."

"In . . . in what?" gasped Vinton. "In your hands?"

"Sure. Bring him forward, men!"

A couple of deputies pushed ahead of the Lone Ranger and Tonto. Between them stood Captain Skinner, a sadly disheveled-looking man, with false mustache askew. But he stood poised and calm. He faced Vinton with loathing in his face. "You," he said in his smooth voice, "are a rat! The way I planned the whole thing, didn't call for the murder of that poor old man. My plan didn't call for murder at all! You thought, you and Brady, that you could double-cross me, and get the gold for yourselves. When you saw that wouldn't work, you went through with the plan as I outlined it!"

"How did they get you?" asked Vinton.

"That Indian dragged me out of the window last night. He saw me putting fresh glue on the mustache, then he knew that the masked man's ideas were right, so he dragged me away. THEY knew who I was."

Potter chuckled at the dismay in Vinton's face. "The masked man planted that shovel that Judge Bellows muddied up fer him, in Tuttle's place . . . in the room he'd rented as Captain Skinner. You coyotes thought he'd double-crossed yuh, an' you couldn't rest till you come here to see if the gold was gone. The masked man figgered whoever was Tuttle's pards would do that same. He suspicioned you two, but he wasn't sure till now."

Vinton broke in again, "Then that's what Bellows was doin'!"

"Course it was. Now if you ain't got any more questions, we'll throw you in jail till time to hang yuh!"

Brady reeled drunkenly for a moment, and then dropped, unconscious, into the six-foot pit. Captain Skinner, or more properly, Dick Tuttle, looked down with contempt. "Yellow-livered coward!" he spat disgustedly. "Go on, Sheriff, throw the dirt in on him and leave him there."

Bannerman turned to Tuttle. "I'm sorry, Tuttle, that you're in on this. I thought I could size up a man, but you sure had me fooled." He sighed slightly, "I liked you."

"I made a mistake, Bannerman, but take my word, I did not plan a murder. That was Vinton's part in the whole thing. I was going to see that he paid for it, as soon as we got clear of here."

Even now, Dick Tuttle commanded the respect of the other men. True Westerners, they liked to see a man who could take his medicine. Dick Tuttle was prepared to take it. "I played a game and lost," he said simply. "Now there's just one thing I'd like to ask. If you'll grant that favor, I'll confess my part and tell a jury the part those two played. That'll make it much easier to hang us."

"What's your request?" asked Bannerman.

"All three of us will hang?"

Sheriff Potter nodded.

"If it doesn't make any difference, let me be the last. I'd like to see those yellow skunks get theirs first."

The lawman agreed that this might be arranged.

It was quite late that night, when Sheriff Potter, Jack Bannerman and Judge Bellows, now released from prison, stood at the porch of the Judge's home.

"Never chuckled so much in all my life," the Judge

was saying. "I knew, when he showed me that silver bullet, who he was. That's why I helped him out."

"You took a doggone big chance," scolded the Sheriff. "Dad-rat you, Bellows, the crowd might have lynched you for what you done."

"Especially," added Bannerman, "with Vinton in-citin' them."

"Shucks," belittled the portly jurist, "I didn't take half the chance that masked man did, when he went out to FIND you gents. You might have shot him on sight."

"And we might NOT," retorted the Sheriff. "When he rode up from behind us, he held a gun in each hand, an' so did the redskin. And they held them shootin' irons as if they knew how to use 'em."

"If you think the masked man DON'T know how to handle a gun, take a look at the target he put five silver slugs into in the shootin' contest."

"But who," broke in Jack Bannerman, "who in thunder IS he?"

"I knew him in El Paso," began Judge Bellows, but that was as far as he went. Fast hoofbeats broke the night. A big white stallion loomed close, and slid to a halt at the porch. The masked man in the saddle said, "I'm sorry I had to knock you down, Judge Bellows. It was that, or let them shoot you."

"Shucks!" a hearty laugh, "I savvied that, partner.

Now hold on, don't you go away until I ask you just
one thing . . ."

"Yes?"

"You sized Captain Skinner up as Dick Tuttle.
How in tarnation did you do it?"

"I, too, was in disguise you know . . ."

"Sure."

"But I wore a close-clipped mustache. I found out
on a previous occasion that a big one, such as Dick
Tuttle wore, is hard to get used to. It is unhandy
when a man tries to eat. I thought it was false when
I saw Dick Tuttle, with otherwise good table manners, fumble with the mustache."

Unbelieving, the Sheriff called, "Is that all the
clue you had?"

"No. I suspected something further when he posed
as a gambler, yet stood through the entire pistol contest without accepting a single bet. Third, the only
man he gambled with in town, was Vinton. And
there were other things. He was supposed to be a
stranger, in Black River for the first time. Yet, he
dropped the remark that he'd seen many previous
Frontier Day celebrations. I felt quite sure of my facts
then. If Skinner COULD have been Dick Tuttle, it
would account for the shot, AND NO SIGN OF A
WOUNDED MAN. The gold had to be hidden
someplace nearby, and it was most likely to be buried.

When Tonto watched Dick Tuttle through the win dow and confirmed our ideas, the rest all fitted in. You could have made the same deductions, Sheriff."

"Like blazes he could," blurted Bannerman.

"Well, anyhow," Potter defended himself, "even you, Jack Bannerman, got to admit that bein' outsmarted at the swamp by a man like THAT ain't nothin' to be ashamed of."

Bannerman agreed with Potter for perhaps the first time in their respective lives. Judge Bellows started to speak, but his words were chopped by a ringing cry from the masked man. At the voice, the white horse whirled and raced away. The darkness quickly swallowed horse and rider.

"That's how he does," explained the Judge. "Rides off before you can even thank him."

Potter grabbed Judge Bellows' beefy arm. "Now YOU," he barked, "open up and tell us who that masked man is."

Judge Bellows chuckled from the stomach. "You blamed old fool! He's the Lone Ranger! Now he's ridin' to join Tonto, and headin' fer somewhere else, where they's trouble . . . where justice is needed! Now let go my arm an' come on inside. See if you like my cigars and wine as well as the four men last night did."

Just before the trio closed the door behind them, the Lone Ranger's voice carried through the night,

as he shouted in the distance, "Hi-Yo Silver, Away!"
The three men listened till the final echo died away.
Then the door slammed shut.

Be sure to read the next Lone Ranger story:
"The Lone Ranger and the Outlaw Stronghold."